PEACOCK FEATHERS

Amelia Lionheart

3rd Edition – 2014

Amelia Lionheart
Peacock Feathers
978-0-9937493-0-8 softcover
978-0-9937493-1-5 ebook (mobi)
978-0-9937493-2-2 ebook (epub)

The paper used in the publication of this book is from responsible forest
management sources.

Printing
Minuteman Press (Calgary North), Alberta
Information and Sales: info@mmpresscgy.com
Printed & bound in Canada

Other titles in this series:
The Dolphin Heptad
An Elephant Never Forgets
Can Snow Leopards Roar?
The Humming Grizzly Bear Cubs

To,
Michelle + David,
I hope you enjoy
the series!
Michelle, it was lovely
to meet you + chat! I hope you
will write a book (preferably lots)
soon.
Best wishes
for conservation,
☺ Lionheart
11 May, 2019

Website: http://www.jeac

Dedicated to Mum,
Debbie Barbour, Michael Hartnett,
Lushanthi Perera, Varini Perera, Nihal Phillips,
Benita Ridout, Tim Soutar and Celia Webb

ACKNOWLEDGEMENTS

As always, there are many people who have taken an interest in my books. In this third edition of *Peacock Feathers* I would like to thank the same wonderful people who assisted me with the publication of the first and second editions and set my feet on the path to becoming a published author:

Debbie Barbour, Joanne Bennett, Mary Anna and Warren Harbeck, Michael Hartnett, Grace and Hubert Howe, Lushanthi Perera, Varini Perera, Gladys Phillips, Nihal Phillips, Robin Phillips, Sandeep Puri, Benita Ridout, Tim Soutar, Celia Webb and Vijitha Yapa Publications.

With respect to this third edition, I wish to extend my warmest appreciation to:

Glenn Boyd, for handling the printing of the books and production of all marketing materials, in his consistently exceptional and efficient manner;
Michael Hartnett, who continues to provide unfailing know-how, encouragement and business advice;
Sarah Lawrence for her advice, support and dedication in bringing these new editions, and the new book, to publication;
Elaine Phillips, my cheerful editor, who proofread the pre-print publications, yet again, with joy and enthusiasm;
and last, but not least, **my family and many friends**, for their encouragement and support.

Once more, a simple but heartfelt **thank you!**

YOU
CAN MAKE A DIFFERENCE

You are UNIQUE! This means YOU have special gifts to help change the world. Talk to your parents about ways in which you can recycle or conserve at home. Ask the wonderful folk at zoos and conservations close to you how you can get involved in all kinds of fun and educational activities. Get your friends and neighbours involved. Look up websites for zoos and wildlife conservations, and check out what's going on around the world!

THEME SONG

Jun-ior Environ-menta-lists and Con-ser-vation-ists!

When we think about our world, all the animals and birds
Who are losing their homes day by day
If each person does their part, it will cheer up every heart
So let's take a stand and act without delay!

We've decided we will strive to keep birds and beasts alive
And to make CONSER-VA-TION our theme
We will talk to all our friends, try to help them understand
That our world must come awake and not just dream!

All the creatures that we love, from the ele-phant to dove,
Must be cared for and well protected, too
So all humans, young and old, have to speak up and be **bold**
Or we'll end up with an 'only human' zoo!

Where environment's concerned, in our studies we have learned
That composting at home can be a start
And recycling's very good, each and every person should
Be aware of how we all can do our part.

To the JEACs we belong, and we hope it won't be long
Till our peers and our friends all will say
They believe that con-ser-vation and environ-menta-lism
Is the only way to save our world today!

Will you come and join our band? Will you lend a helping hand?
Though it's serious, it can be great fun!
Tell your friends about it all, let them join up, big and small
And our fight against destruction will be won!

Jun-ior Environ-menta-lists and Con-ser-vation-ists!

ABOUT THE JEACs

The JEACs (*Junior Environmentalists and Conservationists*), a group created by *Amelia Lionheart* in the first book of her series, attempts to enlighten children – through the means of adventure stories – about conservation and environmental issues. The author is delighted that the JEACs, once only a figment of her imagination, have become a reality in recent years.

The JEACs firmly believe that some of the key factors in **saving our planet** are:

- **Participation**
- **Awareness**
- **Co-operation**
- **Education**

****

JEACs' MISSION STATEMENT AND GOALS

We are an international group of Junior Environmentalists and Conservationists who long to **save our planet** from destruction. We will work towards this by:

- educating ourselves on the importance and necessity:

  o of protecting *all wildlife* – especially endangered species – and the techniques used by conservation groups all over the world to reach this goal;

  o of preventing our *global environment* from further damage, and finding out how we can participate in this endeavour;

- creating awareness of these issues among our peers and by sharing knowledge with them, encouraging more volunteers to join our group;

- becoming members of zoos, conservations and environmental groups in our region, actively participating in events organized by them and, through donations and fundraising efforts, contributing towards their work.

Table of Contents

CHAPTER 1

Summer Hols at Last!

'Summer hols – at last! Hurrah!' yelled Rohan excitedly to the porter as he helped load his heavy suitcase into the waiting train.

'Well, well, well! How time flies,' said Bindu with a grin. 'I feel as if it was just yesterday that I got you two boys off the train and put you on the school bus. Are you sure you aren't sneaking out of school early?' He turned to lend Nimal a hand with his suitcase, too.

Rohan and Nimal went to a boarding school in the town of Binjara, located about 1,500 kilometres away from where they lived.

'No, of course not,' chuckled Rohan, who was in high spirits. 'It may seem like a short time to you, but, man, did it ever drag for me. I had to study like crazy for my exams last week.'

'How did it go?' asked Bindu, who had known Rohan and Nimal ever since they were kids.

'Not bad,' said the boy, climbing into the compartment and sticking his head out of the window to chat with him.

'He came first in his class, with an average of 95 percent, and I didn't do too badly either,' panted Nimal, as he stopped to catch his breath after dumping his suitcase onto the train. He continued, as Bindu raised his eyebrows inquiringly, 'I came third in my class by just half a mark, but only got an average of 75 percent. I'm lucky I even got that, because I only studied hard three days before the exam,' he confessed, turning red with embarrassment.

Nimal had an excellent brain but had a tendency to take things easy.

'Well, congrats to both of you,' said Bindu beaming at them. 'I know your parents will be very proud. Oh, you'd better jump in now, Nimal,' he continued, hearing a whistle. 'The train's almost ready to leave.'

Nimal jumped into their compartment, nearly tripping over the strange-looking umbrella with him. 'Hey, yaar, you nearly forgot your umbrella,' he gasped, handing it over to Rohan.

'That's some umbrella,' said Bindu, staring at it curiously. 'I've never seen one like that. Look at that parrot's head for a handle – and two buttons – it sure is interesting. Oh, there's another whistle – time for the doors to close. Have a good trip, boys, and give my regards to your parents and the girls.'

He closed the compartment door as the train chugged slowly out of the station. The boys hung out of the window, waving to the porter till he was a tiny speck on the horizon.

As the train gathered speed, the boys closed their window and leaned back in their seats with contented sighs, gazing out of the window at the verdant grass with scattered flowers and brush, and the myriad trees in the distance.

Rohan had two younger sisters who went to another boarding school, which closed for holidays at the same time as the boys' school. It was 4 p.m. and it would be a couple of hours before the girls joined the train at Minar station.

Their compartment was compact, and since they had to spend a night on the train, there were four comfortable lower and upper berths, and a tiny bathroom – slightly larger than those on an aeroplane. They would reach their destination, Patiyak Station, the following afternoon, and their mother would pick them up.

Rohan was a year older than his cousin. Nimal was an only child whose father was a renowned computer consultant and travelled a great deal for his work, both in India and abroad – and his wife travelled with him. So their base home was at the Patiyak Wildlife Conservation in the North Indian forests where Jim Patel, Rohan's father, was the manager.

Rohan and Nimal's fathers were brothers and the families were very close. Nimal had lived with Rohan's family since he was three years old.

Jim Patel had worked for conservation groups from the time he was in high school; he had taken conservation and environmental studies as his major in university and then specialized in it while doing his master's degree. He and his wife, Dilki, were passionate about their work and determined to create awareness about the exigency for the preservation of not only animals but also forests, jungles and the environment.

India, a vast land, was a country of extremes. Its geography, climate, vegetation, flora, fauna, culture and languages were so diverse that one could almost believe they were in another country when they moved from region to region. Almost every species of wildlife could be found in its jungles and forest areas. However, due to a variety of reasons, including an increase in poaching and mass killing of wildlife, forest officials, conservationists and the government had been forced to acknowledge that there was a crucial need for even more conservation. They therefore not only channelled funds into this field, but set up groups and organizations to create awareness of these issues in the nation. As a result, India now had approximately 100 national parks and some 400 sanctuaries and conservations.

The Patiyak Conservation had been founded 40 years ago and its staff was devoted to the protection of all animals, not only the endangered species. They were also very conscious that the destruction of forests all over the world and the resultant global warming was not only endangering the animals whose habitat it was, but also causing problems with world ecology.

'Is there anything to eat?' asked Nimal after a while. 'I'm starving.'

'You're always hungry,' said Rohan with a grin. 'Guess it's because you're finally growing taller.'

He rummaged around in his knapsack, found a packet of biscuits and handed them over to Nimal.

'Goody!' said Nimal. 'Chocolate chip – my favourite!' He crunched up a biscuit and continued. 'It's okay for you to talk about *my* eating all the time; you do, as well, but you seem to grow taller with the greatest of ease. I hope at least now I'll be taller than Anu. She's six months younger and yet she's been taller for the past two years. It's really bugging me, to say the least.' He tried to look extremely gloomy about this but failed.

'Oh, come off it, chump,' chuckled Rohan. 'I know it doesn't bother you that much. Five foot four inches at thirteen is not bad for a girl – but I doubt she'll grow much more. She's already taller than Mum and in her last email she said she hasn't grown at all in the past year.'

'Well, our dads are pretty tall,' said Nimal hopefully, 'so perhaps I'll also end up being over six feet. You'll make it easily. You're already five foot nine and you're only fourteen.'

Rohan and Nimal looked fairly alike: other than the fact that Nimal was shorter and had thick, black, straight hair which was crew cut, and Rohan's hair was curly and short – both boys had dark brown eyes set wide apart in square faces, sharp features and light brown skin. They were extremely athletic, too, and had started learning karate at school the previous year.

Rohan's eyes twinkled as he took a couple of biscuits. 'I must say there are lots of advantages in being so tall. Very few guys bother me – hey, yaar, don't eat too many biscuits; you'll spoil your dinner. You know the girls will have a smashing meal for us.'

'Don't worry about *my* stomach,' mumbled Nimal, crunching up biscuits as if he hadn't had a square meal in days. 'I could eat all day long and not stop being hungry.' He stuck out his tongue cheekily and continued, 'Also, you needn't try and play "dad" to me just because you're so humongous.'

'You're begging for a wrestle,' growled Rohan, stuffing the last of his biscuit into his mouth and pouncing on Nimal.

They had a great wrestling match and ended up on the floor with Rohan the easy victor. A conductor poked his head into the compartment to see what all the noise was about, grinned, begged them not to make a hole in the floor of the train and went off laughing. He knew them only too well.

The boys settled down to read and finish off the biscuits, Nimal cheekily muttering under his breath at Rohan, 'Like you aren't going to spoil your dinner, Pop', which Rohan merely acknowledged with a grimace.

Their train passed numerous small stations without stopping, but stopped at the Tooku Station to pick up more passengers.

'Chai! Chai! Caffee! Samosas! Pakoras! Faluda! Oranges! Jellebi! Cheap! Very cheap and tasty, too! Buy some wooden crafts, pretty toys and gifts!' yelled various vendors as they walked up and down the platform, attempting to entice the passengers with their wares.

Rohan and Nimal poked their heads out of the window to observe the fun. They loved watching the vendors, in their colourful dhotis and turbans, balancing trays of wares on their heads with the greatest of ease despite the crowds rushing past them, as they pushed their way to the train to bargain with their customers. It was all a great game. The vendors started off with exorbitantly high prices and the customers attempted to beat the prices down to a reasonable amount. On the rare occasion when there was no haggling, it was quite ludicrous to see the disappointed look on the vendor's face – a sale was incomplete unless there was a fair amount of bargaining.

Nimal called out to a vendor wearing a white dhoti and bright orange turban, who was selling beautifully carved, wooden jewellery boxes.

'Bootiful boxes, Sahib,' said the vendor enthusiastically, guessing that Rohan was the older boy and gazing up at him hopefully. 'They make nice present for your mummyji.'

'How much are they?' enquired Rohan.

'Only twenty rupees! Very, very cheap, Sahib,' the vendor replied.

'Too expensive,' interrupted Nimal in pretended horror. He loved bargaining. 'I'll give you five rupees. I want two – one for my mother and one for my aunt.'

'Aiyiyi, small Sahib,' wailed the vendor. 'That is not enough. See this box? It has so many carvings and is very hard making. I do you favour, small Sahib – for you – only pipteen rupees – because you buy two.'

'Still too much,' exclaimed Nimal, shaking his head in mock sorrow. 'They can only be used for jewellery – and they're not very big. Okay – eight rupees.'

'I a poor man, Sahib,' moaned the vendor dramatically, clutching his turban and squinting at them out of the corner of his eyes, thoroughly enjoying the bargaining session, 'I have to give my ten children khana. But since you want for your mummyji and antyji,' he continued, turning to Nimal, 'I will give you special price – only ten rupees each, small Sahib.'

'Still too much,' began Nimal, but just then the train whistled. 'Oh, well,' he continued, 'you are cheating me, but since the train's leaving, I'll take two for twenty rupees. Here you go.'

He gave the vendor the money and got the boxes. The vendor thanked him profusely and went off with a broad grin on his face, content that he had not only made a good profit, but had bargained with someone who knew the rules and played the game well.

The boys continued to look out the window as the train started chugging slowly out of the station.

'Oh, man – see that guy. Wonder if he'll make the train,' exclaimed Rohan suddenly.

He and Nimal watched tensely as an athletic young man came running into the station just as the train was leaving the platform.

'Hey, I think it's Peter – Peter Collins,' said Nimal in excitement.

'You're right, yaar. It is Peter. Gosh, he's going to jump into that last carriage,' said Rohan.

The boys hung out of the train window, watching to see what would happen. Peter threw his suitcase into the carriage and then swung himself in safely.

'Phew – he made it,' said Rohan with a sigh of relief, sinking back on to his seat. 'I wonder why he was so late for the train. It's not like him, since he generally arrives at least twenty minutes early for anything.'

'Must have been an unexpected delay,' said Nimal. 'Oh, well, I guess we'll hear about it sooner or later. We're bound to meet him in the restaurant car tomorrow at breakfast.'

Peter, a young detective, had grown up on the Patiyak Wildlife Conservation. His parents were naturalists who observed animals and birds, and wrote books on them. They were part of the staff of the Conservation and good friends with the Patels. Peter knew the children very well. He had a good sense of humour, loved animals, and did not treat the children like kids, although he was about twelve years older than Rohan. Rohan was determined to be a detective like Peter, and loved listening to details of all the cases he worked on.

'Well, you look like the cat that got the cream,' said Rohan with a chuckle, as Nimal picked up the beautifully carved boxes and gloated over them. 'They sure were a bargain.'

'I know,' said Nimal with a grin. 'They're real beauts, and a great price, too. I saw similar boxes in that big store near school, and you know, they were 30 rupees *each*, yaar.'

'That store's way overpriced,' said Rohan. 'This guy was thrilled to get ten rupees each, and it probably cost him fewer than six to make one.'

'I think he had more fun bargaining with me,' acknowledged Nimal. 'I know I enjoyed it. Do you think my mater and Aunty Dilki will like them?'

'They'll love 'em,' said Rohan with a smile. 'I remember Mum saying she wished she had another box for her trinkets, and this is really *bootiful*, as the man said.'

The train gathered speed and chugged along while Rohan read a book by P.G. Wodehouse and Nimal had a short nap.

'Wake up, sleepy head,' said Rohan a while later, poking Nimal in the stomach with the umbrella.

'Oooh! Leave me alone,' grunted Nimal sleepily. He tried to roll over on the seat, thinking he was in bed, and fell off with a bump.

'Ow!' he yelped.

Rohan chortled as Nimal woke up with a jerk.

'Very funny,' said Nimal sarcastically. 'I'm delighted to be a constant source of amusement to you.'

He picked himself up and sat down on the seat with a groan. 'Why did you wake me anyway? I was having a wonderful dream about an enormous chocolate cake which was made only for me.'

'We're nearly at Minar Station, and I thought you might want the girls to try and believe you didn't spend *all* your time sleeping,' said his cousin. 'Plus, we've got to hide the umbrella for now.'

'Oh, yeah,' said Nimal, rising in a hurry. 'It'll spoil the surprise if they see it right now. They'll want to try out that special button before we get a chance to use it for an occasion. You know, your suitcase is bigger than mine. Do you think the umbrella will fit inside?'

'Let's try.'

They pulled down Rohan's suitcase and opened it.

'Just about fits,' said Rohan happily, placing the umbrella in diagonally. 'That's good, yaar. Once we get home, I'll cover up the second button so they don't notice it, maybe with a piece of tape or a sticker of some sort.'

'That was a great gift you got from that Zambian chap in school,' said Nimal. 'I guess those umbrellas are very common in Zambia – are they?'

'Well, the carved handles are common enough,' said Rohan 'but Omar said his father's factory makes all types of gadgets, mainly for the CID to use in their work, and among them are these types of umbrellas. This was one of a limited number made for the CID, and Omar and his brother managed to get one each. Omar was really generous to give me his. He said he could get another one from his dad.

'That's because you helped him with his English Lit,' said Nimal. 'Hey, we're coming into the station.'

He pulled up the window and poked his head out.

'Can you see the girls?' asked Rohan, quickly shutting his suitcase, putting it back on the luggage rack and joining Nimal at the window.

'Not yet,' said Nimal, craning his neck to see.

The train drew to a standstill, and the usual clatter and noise of the station filled their ears.

'There they are,' yelled Rohan, spotting his sisters. He waved to them, shouting to attract their attention. 'They've seen us. Come on, Nimal.' He ran out of the compartment, jumped off the train and rushed over to hug his sisters.

Chapter 2

A New Member Joins the Family

Nimal followed Rohan out of the compartment and on to the platform, tripping over pieces of baggage and a large Alsatian dog, who was seated on the platform, its tongue lolling out of its mouth.

The dog wagged his tail and gave Nimal a sticky lick. The boy, who was crazy over all animals, immediately fell in love with this dog. It was quite young, jet-black in colour, had an intelligent face, loving brown eyes, and a long, beautiful tail. Nimal patted it and gave it a biscuit, which he found in his pocket. The dog gobbled it up and pranced around Nimal, whining enthusiastically, his tail wagging fast. He was extremely friendly.

Nimal looked around for the owner of the dog, but could not see anyone nearby.

'Nimal! Nimal!' shrieked Gina, the youngest of Rohan's sisters. Nimal turned just as Gina ran up and flung herself at him.

He gave her a big hug, lifting her up into the air. 'How are you, Gina?' he gasped. 'Boy! You nearly knocked me down, and you've become *so* fat!'

'No, I haven't,' squealed Gina excitedly. A tiny, little girl of eight, she was four feet six inches tall, with masses of short, thick, black, curly hair which framed her pixie like face and wide-awake hazel eyes. She was strong and wiry, despite her fragile looks. 'Whose dog is this?' she exclaimed, kneeling down to hug the dog, who was dancing around them, and getting her face well washed with sticky licks.

'I don't know,' said Nimal, 'but I sure wish he were ours.' He turned to greet Anu who had just come up with Rohan.

'Hi, Anu,' he said, giving her a bone-crushing hug.

'Ouch – my ribs,' groaned Anu. 'Huh, I see you've finally beaten me in height, Nimal.' Her hazel eyes, so like Gina's, twinkled in an oval face that often held a dreamy expression. Unlike Gina, her hair was straight and reached her shoulders.

Rohan laughed. 'He's actually an inch taller than you, sis. He's been putting himself on the stretch rack at school for the past three months. Hello,' he added, spotting the dog, 'and whom do you belong to, sir? What a nice dog you are.'

The children fussed around the dog, which enjoyed all the attention. Just then their favourite porter came up to help the girls load their suitcases into their compartment.

'Hi, Kishore,' chorused the children.

'Hello, kids! So, you've finally finished with school for the summer,' he said, smiling at the excited children. 'And what are you planning to do for fun these holidays? Any trips to the Pink City or the Taj Mahal?'

'Not this year,' said Rohan, grinning at him. 'We're hoping to do some camping instead. Our parents said we could spend as much time outdoors as possible since it is not hot enough to get sunstroke this summer. Plus, it's always great to be out in the open and learn more about the animals and birds that come to the waterholes.'

'True enough,' said Kishore, who also loved animals.

The four children had a deep love for their Conservation Centre, and had grown up on it, learning all about the importance and necessity of conserving the animals and forests. They were an independent group, but enjoyed being together and got along excellently. They ragged each other mercilessly, but let any outsider dare to try and hurt or unfairly criticize one of them to the others, and they would rise up in immediate defence.

Nimal and Gina were still patting the dog, which did not seem to want to leave them.

'Do you know whose dog this is, Kishore?' asked Nimal. 'He's so friendly.'

'He belongs to me now, but there's a sad story behind him,' began Kishore, as he put the girls' suitcases into their compartment. Rohan, Nimal and Anu helped him, while Gina kept her arms around the dog, which licked her lovingly.

'His name's Hunter, and he's just a year old,' continued Kishore. 'He belonged to a family who lived here until two months ago. They had two children who loved Hunter and he adored them, too. Unfortunately, the children's father got a job in Canada and they had to leave Hunter behind since they weren't allowed to take him with them. They gave him to me knowing I would take care of him, but he hasn't been very happy. In fact, this is the first time I've seen him prance around and wag his tail so much. I think he misses the children a great deal.'

'Poor old Hunter,' said Gina, with tears in her eyes. She hugged the dog and he gave a tiny bark and wagged his tail as if he knew they were talking about him.

'I wonder,' began Rohan, and then trailed off with an embarrassed cough.

'Carry on, Rohan,' said Kishore. 'I've a feeling you and I are on the same wave length.'

'Well,' continued Rohan hesitantly, 'you know we've been longing to get a dog, but felt that since it would be with us the whole time we were on vacation, it would miss us terribly and pine for us when we were in school. But next year my school's starting something new. We can take our pets with us and house them in a special menagerie they're building this summer. That means we can get a dog. Do you think...?' He paused, looking hopefully at the porter.

The others held their breath in anxious anticipation. Hunter seemed to know what was happening. He trotted solemnly up to each of the children and licked them, then he went up to Kishore, wagged his tail, and looked pleadingly up at him.

Kishore knelt down and took Hunter's face between his hands.

'Yes, old boy, I know you love children and miss them a lot,' he said. He looked up at the children and continued, 'Well, would you like him to be yours? I'm sure he'll be much happier with all of you than with an old bachelor like me.'

'Oooh, yes!' squealed Gina, throwing herself at Kishore and Hunter, and trying to hug both of them at the same time.

The others jumped for joy and crowded around Hunter, Kishore and Gina, banging Kishore on the back in thanks, and patting and hugging Hunter. The Alsatian barked his head off as if he couldn't agree more with the decision.

The train whistle blew loudly; the children – and Hunter – jumped hurriedly into their compartment, leaning out of the window to say goodbye to Kishore.

'Thanks a ton!' said Rohan gratefully, shaking Kishore's hand vigorously. The others all shook his hand, too, including Hunter, who put out his paw. 'We'll take good care of him, we promise.'

'I know you will,' said Kishore, beaming with satisfaction. He patted Hunter's head, which was sticking out of the train window, too, and Hunter gave him a loving lick. 'I'll write to his old family – I know they'll be relieved to hear that he's happy again. Goodbye, Hunter – I'm sure I'll see you often. By the way, kids, he's an exceptionally well-trained dog, but he does a few funny things – watch out for them.'

'Like what?' began Anu, but just then the train began to move slowly out of the station.

The children waved to the porter and Hunter sent him a farewell bark. Then they all moved away from the window and sat down, Hunter in their midst. It was plain to see that every one of the five was pretty pleased with life.

'Gosh!' exclaimed Nimal, breaking the silence. 'A real dog of our own!' He knelt down and put his arms around Hunter, who immediately licked his face. 'This is superfantabulous!' he continued. 'It's almost too good to be true. Hunter, do you like belonging to us?'

Hunter barked, wagged his tail vigorously and tried to climb up on to Nimal's lap. He seemed to feel that Nimal was his particular buddy since he had seen him first. Also, all animals seemed to have a strange fascination for Nimal, and would willingly let him touch them while shying away from anyone else.

'I'm sure the APs will love him,' said Rohan, 'since they were quite willing for us to have a dog if we could look after him during school term, too. Boy, life is pure bliss just now. Exams over, summer hols, we're all together again, we'll see lots of animals and birds, and best of all, we now have a dog that belongs to us.'

'We can be like the "Famous Five" now that we have a dog,' said Anu brightly. She was a voracious reader and her expression turned dreamy as her imagination took over. 'We can have adventures, catch crooks, visit conservations all over the world, and maybe one day someone will write a book about us. Wouldn't that be fabulous?' Her eyes sparkled as she contemplated this happy future.

'Whoa! Slow down, Anu. Your imagination's running away with you again,' laughed Rohan, and the others chuckled.

They were all used to Anu's vast flights of imagination, and often teased her about it.

Anu smiled. 'One day *I'll* write a book about all of us,' she said, 'and you can bet it'll be a bestseller. Yes, Hunter, you'll be in it, too,' she continued with a laugh, as Hunter pawed her knee and looked up at her.

'He thinks it's funny, too,' said Gina, 'look at him laughing and waving his tail.'

'Where's he going to sleep tonight?' asked Anu. 'I'm sure he won't want to be on the upper berth with one of you boys. Plus he's sticking close to you, Nimal.'

'Oh, please may I have an upper berth this time?' begged Gina. 'I'm not too small now, and I won't fall out. Please, pleeease, Rohan?'

'Well, I guess you could sleep on an upper berth,' said Rohan. 'After all, you're much taller now and it should be okay.'

'Then I'll sleep on one of the lower berths,' said Nimal immediately, 'and Hunter can sleep with me. That'll be great. I've always longed for a dog at the foot of my bed.'

'Good, that's settled then,' said Rohan. 'Now, Anu, where's that wonderful dinner? I'm as hungry as a boa constrictor.'

Hunter immediately jumped up and licked Rohan. 'Down, boy,' laughed Rohan, as he held Hunter's paws and patted the dog. 'I see you take my point of view and understand us completely, old chap – you must be hungry, too.'

Anu rose and opened a large picnic hamper, while the boys pulled down the folding tables in the compartment, and arranged the food as Anu passed it to them.

What a spread there was – a mixture of eastern and western food. There were three different kinds of sandwiches: chicken, tuna and curried mutton mince. There were Punjabi samosas, Chinese rolls, egg parathas, ripe tomatoes, slices of cucumber, cheese and garlic bread. Then there was fruit to follow – sliced mangoes, juicy grapes and watermelon – and nice, cold lemonade to wash the meal down. But best of all was the large chocolate cake for dessert.

'Yummy!' slurped Nimal, licking his lips. 'My dream come true! I'm sure none of you others will want cake after eating all these other goodies.'

'Of course we will,' yelled Gina promptly. She loved chocolate cake almost as much as Nimal did. 'Here are the plates and cups.'

'And here's the salt, pepper and serviettes,' said Rohan, handing them out from the hamper.

'Now for a feast,' said Anu. 'Boy, did we ever have a hectic time getting it all ready this morning.'

'Are you trying to tell me that you and Gina did all that work?' asked Nimal teasingly. 'I thought you couldn't make a decent sandwich to save your life.'

He ducked as Anu threw a serviette at him.

'Well, believe it or not,' she said, 'I did make some of the sandwiches, and I also cooked the mince curry. I wouldn't want to cook all the time but occasionally it's kind of fun; and the matron at our school is great at helping out and getting all the provisions together. Plus,' she added, 'the joy of knowing that next time it's you boys who'll be bringing the meal made it doubly enjoyable.'

'Which sandwiches did you make,' asked Nimal, 'just so I can avoid eating them?'

'Okay, Nimal, dry up and let's eat,' said Rohan, who was already serving himself. 'I'm starving.'

They settled down to a delicious meal, and of course Hunter joined in eagerly and had more than enough food.

When they got to the fruit, Rohan noticed Hunter sit up extremely straight.

'Huh, wonder what's with him?' said Rohan, looking at the dog curiously.

'Maybe he doesn't like fruit,' said Gina.

'I think he does,' said Nimal thoughtfully. 'Let's see what he does with a grape.'

He threw Hunter a big, juicy grape, and then they all gaped in amazement.

Hunter picked up the grape, chewed for a minute and then spat out all the seeds. After this he licked his lips and looked up at the children hopefully.

After a stunned silence, the children burst out laughing and gave him more grapes. He ate them in the same way as the first grape.

'This must be one of the strange habits Kishore was talking about,' chortled Rohan. 'What a dog! I'd love to find out how he learned to do that and why.'

'Wonder what he'll do with a slice of watermelon,' said Gina. 'Here, Hunter – do you like watermelon?' She gave him a small slice.

Hunter took the whole piece of watermelon into his mouth.

'Oooh – he's going to eat it, seeds and all,' squealed Gina.

But as the children watched, Hunter carefully spat out all the seeds from his piece of watermelon. Then he licked his chops and waited for another slice.

'He's incorrigible,' chuckled Nimal, patting Hunter enthusiastically. 'You're certainly a smart chap, aren't you?'

Hunter barked in agreement, looked at the chocolate cake, and sat up and begged.

'Oh, no! Not *another* chocolate cake fanatic!' groaned Anu. She picked up a knife and cut five big slices of the cake. 'Yes, you can have your very own slice, Hunter,' she said.

The dog licked her hand, as if to say thank you, waited till she put the slice down for him and then gobbled it up.

The others tucked into the cake, too.

'Mmmm, delicious,' mumbled Nimal, as he picked every crumb off his plate. 'May I have another piece, please? The same size would suit me fine.'

'Me, too,' said Gina, 'but not such a big piece. I'm getting kind of full now.'

'A piece all round?' asked Anu, and when the others nodded, she cut some more cake and handed it out.

Of course Hunter got his fair share, too, and ate every bit of it. Nimal gave him some water to drink, and then they cleared the tables. They put all recyclable material into separate bags which they would dispose of at home – serviettes and paper cups in one bag; crusts and rinds of fruit in another.

'What a hungry crowd we were,' said Rohan rubbing his stomach contentedly. 'I thought there'd be enough for two meals at least. Those sandwiches were great, Anu. In fact, all the food was yummy.'

'Yeah, even I have to admit that the sandwiches were almost as good as the ones Aunty makes,' teased Nimal.

'Well, thank you all,' said Anu. 'Gina helped to cut up the cucumber and beat the eggs for the cake.'

'You don't mean to tell me you made the cake, too?' gasped Nimal, pretending to be shocked. 'Oh, Anu! Can I come and live with you forever? You're such a fantastic cook.' He went down on his knees, clasped his hands together and looked up at Anu pleadingly.

'Get lost, Nimal,' laughed Anu, who was quite used to her cousin's idiotic ways. 'If you keep eating the way you do, you'll turn into a massive, circular ball.'

'Ball? Moi?' asked Nimal, rising to his feet and gesticulating dramatically in imitation of a comedian he had seen recently in a movie. 'How can you say that to me? Slim and suave as I am. I am, after all, your favourite male cousin.'

'My *only* male cousin,' interrupted Anu grinning, 'and thank goodness for small mercies. What would I do if I had to put up with more chaps like you? You're the giddy limit.'

'Okay, you two,' said Rohan laughing at the comedians, as Nimal pretended to choke Anu and she pulled his hair. 'The two of you should be on stage. Now, shall we play a game, or do you want to do your own thing?' He was the acknowledged leader when all of them were together.

'A game! A game!' chimed Gina. 'Let's play Snap!'

'Okay with you two?' asked Rohan, looking at Nimal and Anu. They nodded.

'Sure, why not,' said Nimal obligingly. 'Where are the cards?'

'I have some,' said Anu, reaching into her knapsack.

The children played a riotous game of cards, with Hunter giving a small bark each time one of them yelled 'Snap!' He got so excited at one point that he jumped up on to Nimal's lap, jumbling up the cards, and they had to stop the game because they were laughing so much that they couldn't concentrate.

'Gosh – what a crazy dog you are, Hunter,' said Nimal, giving him a hug. 'I'm so glad we have you.'

Hunter licked his face, and then went round to lick the others, too, in case they felt left out.

As it grew dark outside, Rohan turned on the lights in the compartment, drew down the shutters of the windows, and locked the door.

'Shall we get the berths ready?' he suggested. 'It's nearly 10 o'clock, and Gina looks half asleep.'

'Good idea,' agreed Anu.

Nimal and Rohan, being the tallest, got the two top berths ready. Gina and Rohan would sleep in those, while Anu and Nimal would have the two lower ones.

'Come on, Gina,' said Rohan, 'I'll help you up and tuck you in if you like.'

'I don't need to be tucked in or helped up, thanks,' said Gina, grinning at her brother. She bent down to give Hunter a hug and a goodnight kiss. 'I'm *so* glad you belong to our family,' she told him, and Hunter barked in agreement.

A moment later, she was up in her berth and feeling very pleased with herself. She was soon fast asleep.

The others snuggled on to their berths, chatting desultorily for a while and gradually dozing off.

Hunter climbed on to the berth with Nimal and heaved a sigh of contentment. He was so happy to be with children once more. He felt that he was of use again – he would look after these friends, and nobody would be allowed to harm them. He had a special feeling for Nimal, and licked his foot gently without waking the boy. Then he, too, drifted off to sleep, to dream of large rabbits that turned into chocolate cake.

CHAPTER 3

A Challenge

Anu was the first to wake up the next morning. She rolled up the window blind and lay on her berth, looking out at the beautiful sunrise. Glancing at her watch she saw that it was only 6 a.m. 'I'll let the others sleep a little longer,' thought the girl, gently pushing up the window and breathing in the fresh air. Hunter opened his eyes and wagged his tail at her, but did not disturb Nimal.

The train was winding its way up some low hills, chugging along slowly, and they were passing through a beautiful area. The tracks followed the curves of a wide, shallow river, lined with rocks and ferns. Anu could see the glimmer of fish as they leapt out of the water at intervals. The grass on the banks of the river was a rich, fresh, green, and was covered with daisies and innumerable other wild flowers nodding in the light breeze. She could even see dew on the fine blades of grass, and a few butterflies were already sipping daintily at the flowers. On the other side of the river there were more hills, covered with beautiful flowering shrubs and dark green trees. A herd of deer gazed at the train from a safe distance.

The scenery was so beautiful that Anu could not resist getting off her berth and fetching her camera from her knapsack to take a few photographs.

'I wish I could draw or paint,' she sighed to herself. 'Maybe I'll just note this in my journal and write about it one day. The pictures will help.'

Rohan peered over the edge of his upper berth. He had been half asleep but woke up fully when he heard the camera clicking. He grinned at Anu and descended carefully, without making a sound. Anu moved over on her berth as he joined her, and they both drank in the magnificence of the panorama unfolding before them. It was absolutely stunning.

Rohan took some pictures too, and got some really good ones as the sun rose above the hills, turning everything into gold and crimson, and making the dew sparkle like diamonds.

The train crawled to a halt at a hillside station called Faizipur, and a number of people got off. This spot was famous for its beauty. The deer, roaming around the area freely, were so tame that they would come up and take food off your hand. It was a popular tourist area, and there were numerous hotels and guest houses around.

The usual bustle of a station woke Nimal, and he yawned sleepily. Rohan and Anu had washed and dressed by then.

'Where are we?' asked Nimal, getting off the berth and stretching.

'At the Faizipur station,' said Rohan.

Hunter got off the berth and licked Nimal. Then he padded over to greet Rohan and Anu, and they fussed over him while Nimal got ready.

'Rohan, it's 7:30 – maybe we should wake Gina now,' said Anu. 'We should go over to the restaurant car in half an hour for breakfast.'

'Gina! Gina! Time to rise and shine,' said Rohan, gently shaking the little girl who was buried under the sheets.

Gina rolled over and blinked at Rohan. 'I'm hungry,' she said, as Rohan helped her down from the berth.

Rohan laughed, 'You and Nimal are always hungry,' he said. 'Well, if you hurry and get dressed, we can go and have something to eat. Also, we forgot to mention it last evening, but Peter's on the train and I'm sure he'll join us.'

Gina stopped to say hello to Hunter who was jumping up at her, and then quickly got washed and dressed. Anu put away the bed linen while the boys put up the berths. The train moved out of the station and the children gazed out of the window for a while.

'Well, time to go and get seats for brekker,' said Rohan, looking at his watch. 'It's nearly 8 o'clock.'

'I hope they have eggs and sausages,' said Nimal hungrily. 'Come on, Hunter. Grub time.'

'It's a good thing they send the bill direct to Dad, Nimal,' said Anu with a mischievous grin. 'We wouldn't have enough money to pay for the amount of food you eat.'

The boy made a face at her as he locked their compartment, and they walked down the corridor to the restaurant car. They were the first people in the restaurant.

'Jacob! Jacob! It's us,' called Gina to the head waiter whom they knew well.

'Oh, no! Not you hungry bunch again,' said Jacob, clutching his head and groaning. 'I guess we'll just have to let the rest of the train starve once more.'

'You *always* say that,' said Gina, as everyone laughed, 'but I haven't seen anyone starving yet.'

Jacob, who had four sons in their teens, was quite used to large appetites.

'And who's this?' he said, spotting Hunter who was standing behind the children.

'This is Hunter,' said Nimal. 'Sit, Hunter, and shake with a friend.'

Hunter sat down and waved his right paw in the air towards Jacob. Jacob shook it and patted the dog.

'I'm impressed! Where did you get him?' he asked, leading them to a table by a large window.

Rohan told him the story and Jacob was delighted since he knew the children had been longing for a dog.

'Will your parents mind?' asked Jacob.

'Oh, no!' said Anu, 'The APs were quite in favour of us having a dog, but concerned as to who would take care of it when we went back to school.'

'APs?' asked Jacob, 'What are those?'

'Oh, sorry,' said Anu with a laugh, 'I mean "Aged Parents". That's what we call them amongst ourselves and they don't mind even when we say it in front of them.'

Jacob chuckled. 'You do come up with some strange phrases,' he said. 'I don't hear many kids speaking as you do.'

'I guess it's because we read so much,' smiled Anu. 'Also, since we not only read a lot of the classical literature our parents used to read, but also contemporary Indian, British and a number of American authors – and of course any other books we can get hold of – our lingo is a mixture of formal and colloquial.'

'It certainly is. Well, good for you,' said Jacob. 'I guess one could say that you are world citizens – at least where literature is concerned.'

'Jacob, do you mind setting an extra place for our friend Peter?' asked Rohan. 'We know he's on this train and he normally comes in for breakfast. We'd love to have him sit with us.'

'Sure thing,' said Jacob, setting another place, 'and now,' he continued, beaming at the children, 'what would each of you like? There's egg bhujia, sausages, cheese, fried onions and tomatoes, lots of hot buttered toast, and different kinds of jam. There's also tomato chutney which tastes great with the egg bhujia.'

'Oooh! What a choice!' said Nimal hungrily. 'I'll have a large plate with some of each, please.'

Jacob joined in the laughter over Nimal's appetite, but as the idea was a good one, the others decided to have the same and ordered for Peter, too, since they knew what he liked. Jacob went off to place their order and find a big bowl of food for Hunter, after seating some other passengers.

'There's Peter,' said Rohan, spotting the young man as he came into the car.

Peter saw the children and immediately walked over to join them.

'Hey! What a pleasant surprise to meet all of you on this train,' said Peter with a broad grin as he hugged the girls and shook hands with the boys. 'Do you mind if I join you for breakfast?'

'Of course not,' they chorused.

Peter sat down as Rohan said, 'We asked for a larger table so that we could sit with you.'

'How did you know I was on this train?' asked Peter in surprise. 'I didn't see you at any of the stations – though I must confess I didn't look out as I was busy doing a report on my computer, which had to be emailed off to my boss last night.'

'We saw you run into Tooku station at the last minute, and just about miss the train,' said Rohan. 'How come you were so late for it?'

'Well,' began Peter and then stopped as a polite bark was heard. He peered under the table and saw Hunter. 'And whom do we have here?' he said.

'Oh, sorry, that's Hunter,' said Nimal. 'Hunter, shake. This is one of our best friends.'

Hunter waved his right paw in the air and looked up at Peter. Peter shook his paw and patted Hunter on the head. He, too, loved dogs.

'What a beauty he is,' said Peter after he had fussed over Hunter. 'How did you get him? He seems like a very intelligent dog – he didn't even growl when I sat down.'

'I guess he recognized from our tones that you were a friend and wanted to greet you,' said Rohan. 'He's smart, and man, does he ever have some queer habits.'

The children took it in turns to tell Peter the story of how they got Hunter and the strange manner in which he ate grapes and watermelon. Peter was thoroughly amused and very pleased for them and the dog.

Their breakfast arrived and they tucked in hungrily. Hunter was given a special bowl with sausages and biscuits, and of course everyone gave him bits and pieces from their own plates. It was a delicious meal, and they ate in silence for a while, gazing out of the windows at the changing landscape. They were now passing through dense forests and the trees were getting closer together and taller. There was also a fair amount of underbrush, and every now and then they spotted small animals like rabbit, deer and jackals pausing in their search for food to watch the train from a safe distance.

As they waited for second rounds of food, Rohan said, 'You were about to tell us why you were so late for the train, Peter.'

'Oh, yeah,' said Peter. 'Where shall I begin?' He thought for a moment and then said, 'You know about the problem the Conservation has been having with peacock poaching?'

The children nodded. They were aware that, for the past month, poachers had been killing peacocks, and Rohan's parents were very concerned about this but had not had much luck in catching the crooks.

Peter continued, 'Well, last week even more peacocks were killed. Three birds were stripped of all feathers and just left to rot near one of the waterholes; the others were found in various parts of the jungle, also without their feathers. There wasn't even any attempt to bury the poor creatures.' Peter's voice growled in anger.

The children were horrified and Anu and Gina had tears in their eyes. They all hated the idea that anyone could be so cruel as to kill animals or birds in the first place, and then just leave them to rot like that. It was appalling.

'That's disgusting and horrid!' said Anu passionately. 'Why are people so horrible? How would they like it if someone did that to them?'

'Over how many days did this go on,' asked Rohan sharply, 'and were all the birds killed at the same waterhole?'

'Well, the birds were found within a week, and we think they were killed at waterholes located in the northern area of the Conservation – within walking distance of each other,' said Peter, 'but we're not quite sure.'

'How come Uncle and his staff were unable to catch the fellows?' asked Nimal furiously.

'They've tried everything they could,' said Peter, 'but you know how large the Conservation is and not too many of the staff can leave their other work to cover fifteen to twenty waterholes each night. Though the waterholes are in the same location, it would take a minimum of twenty minutes to get from one to the other. Also, the poachers are very cunning and clever; they seem to know exactly where to hit next without being caught. And because the weather has been so dry lately, they don't even leave any footprints.'

'So what's happening now?' asked Rohan. 'I'm sure Dad won't give up that easily.'

'Well, that's the reason I was late for the train,' said Peter. 'Your dad called my boss last morning and asked if I could be sent to deal with this problem as a special case. My boss knew that I loved the Conservation and the animals, and realized that I was very keen on dealing with this situation and catching those crooks. I was wrapping up a case in Tooku yesterday afternoon, and since I had just been assigned to help with another case in Hardwar, he felt that I could handle this one, too, since Hardwar is so close to Patiyak. So he called me up and told me to get on the case. I had twenty minutes to catch the train. The Tooku police station used a police car with a siren to get me to the station in time. And so, here I am.'

Peter was well respected in the force, and had risen rapidly in the ranks.

'Wow! That's great, yaar,' said Nimal. 'I'm sure if anyone can catch those crooks, you can. Did you bring all your detective gear, too?'

'You mean like my raincoat, magnifying glass and violin?' asked Peter, grinning broadly.

'No, of course not,' said Nimal with a chuckle. He had also read about Sherlock Holmes, the famous detective. 'I meant your kit for taking finger prints, a gun, your portable computer with email facilities and all that kind of high-tech stuff.'

'Yes, of course, but I need those more for my other case,' said Peter. 'However, I'm hoping that a certain group of young people I know will assist me. What do you say? Will you have time to help me with this case? I could use five bright sparks like you.'

He looked around the table at the eager children and raised his eyebrows questioningly.

'Of *course* we'll help. You'd have a tough time trying to keep us out,' exclaimed Rohan excitedly. This was the first time Peter had worked on a case in their vicinity, and Rohan was thrilled that they may be of some help to him. He would get hands-on experience as a detective, too.

The others nodded fervently, while Hunter whined excitedly – he knew something was being planned.

Gina slipped her little hand into Peter's and sobbed, 'We *won't* go back to school till we catch those crooks. They are mean and wicked.' She was most distraught.

'What's up, Gina?' asked Jacob, as he returned with their second order of food and looked at the little girl in concern.

'She's upset because of all those peacocks which are being killed, Jacob,' said Peter, giving Gina a consoling hug.

They told Jacob what was happening on the Conservation and he was most indignant.

'But why peacocks?' asked Jacob.

'Because,' explained Rohan, 'these beautiful birds – especially the Indian Blue peacock – are often caught and exported to traders looking for exotic birds to sell; or they're killed for their feathers. There's an enormous market, both in India and abroad, for ornaments, fans, decorations, jewellery, masks and head dresses, which are some of the things made out of peacock feathers. They fetch great prices and anyone who can supply the dealers with these feathers will make a lot of money.'

'It's wicked to *kill* them just because people want to decorate their homes with feathers,' said Anu angrily. 'If they want feathers, they should collect the ones that drop off.'

'But why don't the birds fly away?' asked Jacob. 'Is it because they're too big?'

'No, they are able to fly up into very tall trees if they want to,' said Nimal. 'But some of them are so tame that they even come into the areas where our guest bungalows are. They love cars – especially new and shiny ones – and will stand on top of them with their tail feathers all fanned out, and dance. They love human attention.'

'I've heard that they're very noisy,' said Jacob, interestedly. 'Is that true? They're so beautiful that I can't imagine them being noisy.'

'Actually, they make the weirdest sounds,' said Rohan, 'almost human sounding at times. Sometimes the peacocks call out "Helllp! Helllp!" or shout "Ohhh! Ohhh!" The peahens sound a bit different, almost like a "Helll-o!" It's quite fascinating.'

'And when the males dance, with their feathers fanned out – especially if there's a full moon – they call out, "Aaahhh! Aaahhh!"' added Nimal with a grin. 'They do this to attract the females so that the peahens will come and admire them.'

'Well, I certainly hope you catch the crooks fast,' said Jacob. 'Good luck!'

'Thanks, Jacob, we'll do our best,' said everyone.

Jacob went off and Peter turned to the children again. He raised his cup of coffee and said, 'Well, here's to all of you. May you solve "The Case of the Peacock Feathers" really quickly.'

The children cheered and Hunter joined in with a bark.

'Unfortunately, I'd better go back to my carriage and catch up on a bit of reading on my cases,' said Peter, when they had finally finished their meal. 'Let's meet at my place tomorrow morning, at 7 sharp; I'll go over the details of this case with you, and we can then decide what immediate steps should be taken. Any suggestions from you lot would be most welcome,' he added.

'Okay, that sounds great,' said Rohan. 'We'll discuss it when we go back to our compartment and let you know what we come up with. By the way, how are you getting back to the Conservation this afternoon? The mater is coming to pick us up, in the Jeep, and there'll be enough room for you, too.'

'Thanks, but no thanks, yaar,' said Peter. 'I have to check in on the Hardwar case first, and one of my colleagues will be waiting to pick me up from the station and take me there. I'll be dropped off at home later on tonight.'

Hardwar was about 100 kilometres away from Patiyak.

'How are you going to work on the two cases simultaneously?' asked Anu interestedly.

'Well, I'm hoping that I can leave you five with various instructions and information as to what to look out for at the Conservation, and I'll be checking back with you on a regular basis. In fact, knowing that you would be home for the hols, and would probably spend most of your time out of doors, I told my supervisors that I had some good folk who could help me with the peacock feathers' case. They were jolly pleased when I told them about you folks because they knew that the Patiyak case would be in good hands. I'll be based at the Conservation, but depending on how the other case progresses, I may have to be away for a few days at a time. However, I'm confident that you can deal with certain aspects of the case as well as, in fact better than, I can,' said Peter matter-of-factly.

'We'll certainly do our best to catch those crooks,' said Rohan resolutely.

They all got up from the table, thanked Jacob, and trooped off, Peter returning to his carriage and the children and Hunter going back to theirs.

The youngsters did not speak till they were in their compartment and had closed the door. Then they sat down and looked at each other in excitement.

What a challenge! Of course they were going to solve 'The Case of the Peacock Feathers' and save their beloved birds from being destroyed.

CHAPTER 4

The Junior Environmentalists and Conservationists (the JEACs)

'Wow! Here we go! A mystery to solve – on our very *own* Conservation,' said Anu, breaking the silence at last. 'You know, I think we should start a group.'

'What kind of group, Anu?' asked Gina curiously. 'A club that solves mysteries?'

'No, Gina – not really – though we could do that, too. I mean a group to make others aware of environmental and conservation issues – a junior group,' said Anu. 'We could be the founding members, and then at school, we could try and get others to join in and create awareness among the people they mix with. What do you think?'

'Brilliant, Anu,' exclaimed Nimal at once. 'We could get some more ideas from the APs, and perhaps that way we could start a new generation of folk – eager to save our world.'

'I agree entirely,' said Rohan thoughtfully. 'We have, as far as I know, no junior group like that in India. And maybe, via the internet, we could start inviting others to join us.'

'Wow – can I belong, too?' asked Gina eagerly.

'Of course you can,' said Anu promptly. 'Anyone who loves animals, birds and nature, and is concerned about the environment, can join. Now, what shall we call ourselves?'

'The "Young Environmentalists" something or other?' queried Rohan.

'How about the "Junior Conservationists"?' said Nimal.

They tossed around a few other suggestions, but nothing clicked.

'I know,' said Anu suddenly, 'let's use a combination of the first two ideas – how about – "The Junior Environmentalists and Conservationists"? We could call ourselves the "JEACs" for short.' (She pronounced it 'Jee-acks' with a soft J as in 'Jeep'.)

'Perfect, just perfect,' agreed the others happily.

'So, JEACs, whenever we get a chance, probably once we've solved the problem of the peacocks, we'll ask the APs for some ideas, and put together a mission statement, goals and objectives. We'll also draft a "Mandate" so that others know what the requirements are in order to start a group of JEACs, and what types of organizations we will fundraise for,' continued Anu.

They were all familiar with the way in which groups were set up since Mrs. Patel had started up a conservation group for adults. They discussed plans eagerly for a while.

'Okay, this is great,' said Rohan. 'I'm sure the APs will be only too pleased to hear our news. Now, perhaps we had better think about the peacock case.'

'Yeah,' said Nimal. 'That'll be an adventure to say the least.'

The others laughed, but they were all equally thrilled at the prospect of having an adventure. Rohan, in particular, could not believe his luck in having a real case to work on for the first time. They spent the rest of the morning discussing the case, and thinking of all the ways in which they could catch the crooks.

'I think we should take our sleeping bags, binoculars and other gear, and go down to our cave near the biggest waterhole. It's in the area of the peacock killings and we know that peacocks frequent that waterhole regularly. Also there are several other smaller waterholes close to it, and we can keep an eye on all of them. That'll leave Dad and the others free to cover the balance waterholes and still be able to look after the rest of the Conservation,' said Rohan, writing rapidly in a little notebook he found in his knapsack. 'Our cave is really well hidden by those thick bushes and no one can see us get in or out. If we spend a few nights there, someone is sure to catch the guys.'

'And I hope it's us. I think that's a great idea, Rohan,' said Nimal enthusiastically. 'We can also take your umbrella, just in case, and buy some of the other things we'll need for a longer stay – like lanterns, a tiny cooker, some pots and pans, and other paraphernalia.'

'An umbrella?' quizzed Anu in surprise. 'I've never in my life known you to carry an umbrella anywhere, Rohan. What kind of an umbrella is this?'

'Wait and see,' said Rohan mysteriously. 'It's the most extraordinary umbrella in the world, and it could save our lives.'

'Oh, yeah. I know you and your suspense stories, Rohan,' said Gina sceptically. 'You just want to make us curious. It's probably a simple umbrella. Anyway, Rohan, do you think we can take Hunter to the cave, too? I would hate to leave him behind.'

'Oh, I don't think there'd be any problem at all with him,' said Rohan immediately. 'He's well trained, and he'd be a great guard dog and could warn us of any danger. He can easily slip through the tree trunk tunnel with us.'

'It's so deceptive, isn't it?' said Anu thoughtfully. 'To anyone watching us from the waterhole or the opposite side, it looks as if we just went behind the tree, through the bushes, and carried on up the trail.'

'Yeah,' agreed Nimal, 'while in actual fact we go through the covered hole in the tree, into the tunnel and up into our cave. Boy! We're lucky the tunnel is so big, otherwise Rohan wouldn't fit in it any longer.'

'And it's all because of me that we found it,' chirped Gina gleefully. 'If I hadn't discovered it that day while we were playing hide-and-seek, we wouldn't have such a great place to hide in.'

'Right on, Gina. I'm also glad, given the current situ that we covered up the large hole in the tree with even more bushes. It's not at all noticeable now, and no one else knows about it, except us,' said Rohan. 'I think I'll take the walkie-talkie set I got a few years ago,' he continued. 'Unfortunately, a mobile phone would be useless as we wouldn't be able to plug it in for charging. The range of the walkie-talkie isn't too bad and we can use it to keep in touch with each other when we have to go in different directions. I've a sneaky feeling we'll have to split up into pairs quite often, so that we can cover more ground.'

'I'll bring my sketch pad,' said Nimal, who was good at art. 'We might need to make sketches of footprints.'

'Good idea, Nimal,' said Anu, 'and I'll take my camera and get some high-speed film for it in case we have to take snaps at night. I'll take my journal, too, and we'll ask Mum to give us lots of tinned food and other goodies to eat. After all, we can't have you starving, Nimal – your rumbling stomach may give away the show.'

'Very funny, ha ha,' said Nimal scathingly. 'What will you take, Gina?' he asked, turning to the little girl who was deep in thought.

'I think I'll take my flute,' she said slowly. 'You never know, it might come in handy if we meet a snake and I can make it dance to the music. And if not, at least I can practise a bit. I'll also take my binocs and a bag for the clues.'

None of the others made fun of her since they did not want to hurt her feelings. However, as they were well aware, it was just a myth that snakes 'danced' to music. The reality was that while playing a flute, snake charmers generally swayed to the music. Snakes instinctively observed movements, and so they swayed along with the charmer. Also, fortunately for the children, the particular area they would be in did not have poisonous snakes – just harmless ones which preferred to move rapidly out of the way of any danger rather than stay and confront it.

'Time to pack up our things,' exclaimed Rohan suddenly noticing the time. 'We'll be at the Patiyak Station in fifteen minutes, so hurry, everyone. I wonder what Mum will think of Hunter?'

They bustled about, packing everything away, and making sure that they had not left any garbage in the compartment. The train was slowing down, and as it drew into the Patiyak Station, the four children and Hunter put their heads out of the window to look out for Mrs. Patel.

'There she is!' screamed Gina in excitement. 'Mum! Mum! We're here!'

The others spotted her and waved madly, too.

Mrs. Patel waved back merrily. The train came to a screeching halt and the four children and dog tumbled out of the compartment. The children rushed over to Mrs. Patel, all trying to hug her at once. She laughed as she hugged them back.

They all talked at the same time, and she tried to answer their rapid-fire questions.

'Whoa!' she said at last. 'Rohan, remember how big and strong you are now, and don't crack my ribs with your bear hugs.'

'Sorry, Mum,' said Rohan grinning, 'It's just that it's so good to see you and be home again.'

'Mum,' said Anu, 'I want to know if you've finished the cookery book you were writing. I need some recipes.'

'Do you mean to tell me you actually want to cook, instead of read and write?' teased her mother. 'Sorry, hon, but the book is only half complete at the moment – I've been busy.'

'Anu made a great chocolate cake,' cried Gina excitedly, 'and I helped, too.'

'I can see you are all full of news,' said Mrs. Patel smiling around at the children. 'Save some of it for when your dad's around, as well. Nimal, I do believe you have grown a lot since I last saw you at Christmas – are you taller than Anu now?'

Nimal's height was a standing joke in the family since he was so conscious of it all the time.

'Yes, Aunty divine, I am,' said Nimal proudly, 'a whole inch taller. And I'm taller than you, too.'

His aunt laughed as she said, 'I know your dad will be very pleased to hear the good news. You can tell him and your mother tonight over the phone.'

'Great – where are they at the moment?' asked Nimal eagerly. 'The last time they called me was at school early this week, on Tuesday, and they were in Agra on a one week contract of some kind.'

'They had to rush to Delhi,' said Mrs. Patel. 'The prime minister's office was threatened by a computer virus, and your dad was asked to drop everything else and hurry there. He will call from the Inter-Continental Hotel at about ten tonight. They also sent you a large package – a whole trunk, in fact – and it's waiting for you at home.'

'Goody,' said Nimal. 'I'm sure it has some interesting things in it, as usual.'

Hunter, who had held back while the children greeted Mrs. Patel, now felt it was time to present himself to this lady. He could tell that she was someone very special to the children. He remembered how, in his old

family, the lady had petted him a lot when he took her something –
especially a flower. So he went up to a bush containing some tea roses and
pulled one off. Holding in it in his mouth, he pushed through Nimal's legs.
He sat down right in front of Mrs. Patel, whined and waved a paw towards
her.

'And who are you?' asked Mrs. Patel, looking at him in astonishment.
'Is that for me?' she continued as Hunter nosed up to her and held up his
head with the rose in his mouth.

Everyone gaped at this new trick of Hunter's. Mrs. Patel, bent down
and took the flower from Hunter, and then shook his paw and made a big
fuss over him. He wriggled in ecstasy. Mrs. Patel looked around at the
children and said in an amused tone, 'Well, is someone going to tell me the
story about this dog?'

The children stopped gaping and made a fuss over Hunter, too,
praising him and laughing at his funny trick.

'We haven't seen him do that trick before, Aunty,' said Nimal, still
chuckling. 'What an incorrigible dog you are, Hunter,' he continued,
holding on to Hunter's front paws as the dog jumped up at him.

'It was like this, Mum,' commenced Rohan, but just then the porters
came up with their baggage on a trolley, and Peter joined them, too.

'We'll tell you the story on the way home,' said Rohan, 'but he does
belong to us now.'

'Hello, Aunty Dilki,' said Peter, joining the group and greeting Mrs.
Patel with a hug. Although Mrs. Patel was not really his aunt, the families
were so close that he had always called her 'Aunty'.

'Hello, Peter,' said Mrs. Patel. 'I'm so glad they called you in for our
case – your mother gave us the good news this morning. Are you coming
with us now? Mike's longing to meet you.'

'I'm afraid not, but this gang will give you all the details,' said Peter.
'Unfortunately, I have to rush off now – there's a chap waiting for me
outside and he's in a hurry to leave. See you later, Aunty, and would you
mind calling Mum and Mike and telling them that I've arrived safely and
will call them before I leave Hardwar? Thanks. Well, folks, see you early
tomorrow morning.'

'Yes, sir!' said Rohan, snapping to attention and saluting smartly.
'We'll be there, rain or shine!'

The others saluted, too, and Hunter barked and sat up straight, waving his right paw in the air.

Peter laughed, waved goodbye, and rushed off.

'All right,' said Mrs. Patel. 'Shall we head home now?'

Mrs. Patel chatted with the children as they waited for the porters to load their baggage into the Jeep, noticing little changes that had taken place since Christmas. Then they climbed into the Jeep, Rohan sitting in front with his mother.

'All set?' asked Mrs. Patel, starting up the Jeep.

'Yes,' they chorused and Hunter barked in agreement.

They set off. It would take them an hour to get to the Conservation and another 45 minutes, once they were through the gates, to reach their home.

'Well, is someone going to tell me about this lovely dog,' asked Mrs. Patel, 'or am I going to "die of curiosity", as Anu says?'

They laughed and Nimal said, 'Let Anu tell the tale – she always tells a great story.'

So Anu related the tale. She did an excellent job of it, too, leaving out no details and telling it with a great deal of humour.

Mrs. Patel listened in silence, and when Anu was done, said to the boys, 'I'm so glad to hear your school has finally set up a menagerie for pets. Hunter,' she continued to the dog, who had his head over the back of the front seat and was breathing down her neck, 'welcome to the family. We've been waiting a long time to get a nice dog for the children and you are perfect.'

Hunter barked and licked her cheek gratefully. He always seemed to know when he was the subject of the conversation and was being praised.

They drove along chattering nineteen to the dozen. Mrs. Patel was very pleased to have all of them back again. Though she was so busy, she missed their bright conversation and looked forward to having them home during their holidays.

'Your fathers will be pleased to hear how well you boys have done in school – you need good grades for future studies,' she said, when they told her their rankings in class. 'And how did you two girls do?' she asked.

'I came fifth in class,' said Anu, 'and got 95 percent, the highest marks in school for English literature.'

'Good. Anything new about the story writing contest?' asked Mrs. Patel.

'No, nothing just yet,' said Anu, shrugging, 'but they hope to give us details when we return to school.'

The town of Minar, where Anu and Gina went to school was planning to hold a competition for young writers. The school knew about this and was encouraging Anu to write a story for it, but the topics and length of story were not decided on yet, and they had to wait for more information. Anu was quite impatient to start writing.

'Well, what about you, Gina?' asked Mrs. Patel, twinkling at her youngest daughter through the rear view mirror of the Jeep.

Gina caught her eye and smiled sheepishly. 'I didn't do so well in lessons,' she said slowly, 'but I did pass.'

'Just about, I guess,' said Mrs. Patel with a laugh. 'I'm sure you excelled at sports and music, though, didn't you?'

'Oh, yes,' said Gina eagerly, leaning over the back of her mother's seat, 'I got "best sports girl" for my class and will be games captain for the Junior School next year.'

'Good for you – I'm pleased to hear that,' said Mrs. Patel, who had also played a lot of sports in school. 'And what about your music?'

'I can play the flute much better now,' said Gina, who was a talented little musician. 'You know, Mum, I've decided that I want to be a snake charmer when I grow up. One of them came to school and he didn't even play the flute as well as I do. I think I'll be a famous snake charmer and I'll charm cobras and rattle snakes and pythons.'

'Oh, man, and I thought it was Anu, whose imagination ran riot,' teased Rohan.

The others laughed. Gina had been through the stages of wanting to be a nurse, a vet, a doctor, the manager of a conservation, a rock star, an Olympic champion and a zookeeper, but she always wanted her music. The little girl was used to their teasing and she just grinned.

'Mum, I also wrote a limerick,' she said, suddenly. 'Do you want to hear it?'

'Sure,' said her mother. Gina loved writing nonsense verse, particularly in the form of limericks, and was getting to be quite good at it.

'Here goes, then,' said Gina and started to sing.

'There once was a snake-charming chappie,
Who tried to keep all his snakes happy,
He would feed them fat flies, and large apple pies,
Then he'd laugh 'cause they all became snappy!'

Everyone laughed heartily at her latest composition. She had a nice singing voice and was extremely expressive.

'Gina, you're hilarious,' chortled Nimal, giving the little girl a friendly punch. 'Are you going to make up some other poems this summer? Maybe about Hunter's funny habits?'

'I'll try,' said Gina with a pleased grin. She loved making the others laugh.

It was hard, at times, to be the youngest of the lot. The three older ones were all quite academic, and did very well in school. However, she was fortunate in that her parents and the others did not make her feel bad about her lack of academic prowess. They encouraged her to develop her many other talents, and Gina, and her siblings, were gradually learning that being an academic was not the only goal in life. It was more important to do one's best at whatever one undertook.

CHAPTER 5

Home Again

'Well, here we are at the gates to our kingdom!' declaimed Anu dramatically as they approached the staff entrance to the Conservation.

The chowkidar opened the computerized gates by pushing a key on his computer, and then closed them once the Jeep had come through.

'Wow, that's new since Christmas,' said Nimal. 'Did Dad set it up?'

'Of course – who else?' said Mrs. Patel.

The chowkidar came out of his station to welcome the children, looking very smart in his sparkling white dhoti, jacket and white turban. Of course Hunter had to be introduced. The youngsters got out for five minutes to stretch their legs, and then climbed back into the Jeep and moved on towards home.

It was a large conservation, which hosted over 700 species of birds and animals, most of which could be seen at the waterholes. The Conservation, which covered an area of around 900 square kilometres of dense jungle, was divided into two sections: the first section, which covered about 300 square kilometres, was home to many birds and smaller animals such as deer, jackals, wild boar, hare and peacocks; it was known as 'Harmonious Paradise' and called 'HP' for short by all the Conservation folk.

The second section, which covered the rest of the area, was for animals like all the big cats, including the Bengal tigers, Asiatic lions, bears, elephants, giraffes, rhinos, wolves, the gharial (which is a species of fish-eating crocodile) and hyenas; it was called 'Conservationists' Heaven' or 'CH'.

The Patel home was in the first section, and the children were allowed to wander around freely, without supervision, in that area, as long as they were careful.

Though sponsored and supported by government funding, there was never enough money for the implementation of all the improvements that Mr. Patel and his staff would have liked to make at the Conservation. However, they had a group of enthusiastic and dedicated folk, who came up with innovative ideas as to how they could raise money towards meeting their goal of creating awareness on conservation issues, and they progressed slowly but surely.

With Mrs. Patel as the main fundraising organizer, they put into effect many of their ideas. They charged a small entrance fee. Guided tours were held throughout the year, when people could buy tickets and be taken in Jeeps, Land Rovers and minivans for rides around certain areas, to observe the wildlife. Some of these tours were conducted at night so that people could see nocturnal animals at the waterholes; or they could experience the thrill of spending a night in a tree house, watching the tigers and lions, or trek through the jungle on the back of an elephant. There were also areas where they could go and observe some of the young animals who were being hand reared by vets, and see some of the wildlife which had been injured or were being kept under observation for a variety of reasons. As there was no zoo within a 500-kilometre radius of the Conservation, Patiyak was a popular outing for families. It was also a well-known tourist attraction, being a conservation centre with not only the exotic flavour of the East, but also with many of the comforts of the West. Tourists loved to rent out one of the small but well-equipped rest houses and participate in the activities organized for them, eat a variety of Indian foods, and watch the cultural shows that were offered on a regular basis.

Patiyak was also becoming well known for the educational component in all its programmes, and many schools and universities encouraged their students to spend some time at Patiyak as volunteers. There were lectures and film shows led by the Patels, Peter's parents and many of the other staff; Mike Carpenter had specialized not only in conservation issues but also in how to facilitate large group discussions. There was a souvenir shop, a book store, and a couple of cafeterias. During high peak seasons for tourists, dance troupes were invited to hold cultural shows, and many of these troupes donated their talents to the Conservation.

Mrs. Patel was responsible for all the fundraising events that took place to raise money for their work, and the JEACs enjoyed participating in these events whenever they could. Mrs. Patel had founded a membership for volunteers interested in conservation and environmental issues, and was determined to create as much awareness as she could in the country, even though she knew that many people were too poor to contribute monetarily. Mrs. Collins, and several others who lived on the Conservation, helped out with various administrative aspects. It was an extremely taxing task, but they were all devoted to the cause and enjoyed running the campaign programmes, keeping members up to date on the latest news.

The Conservation was quite famous, and people came from all over the world to see it. Rohan, Nimal and Peter's parents, along with the rest of the staff, were always looking for new and innovative ways of providing a safe, healthy, happy environment for the animals and birds. The famous writer/naturalist, Gerald Durrell, had also visited the Conservation to encourage them and give them advice. Unfortunately, Nimal did not get a chance to meet Mr. Durrell, since he was at school when that distinguished gentleman was free to visit the Conservation.

Nimal, who was crazy about anything to do with animals, was determined to become a conservationist/naturalist and protect animals in the wild.

As they drove along the trail, the children fell silent. They loved the dense, green jungle with its enormous trees, the heavy underbrush with its rainbow of colours, the perfume from its summer blossoms mingling in the fresh air. They could see some animals disappear from their path as the Jeep drove along. Birds were all over the place, flashing their brilliant colours and singing from the treetops.

Inquisitive monkeys leapt on to the hood of the Jeep, which now had to travel very slowly, peering in at them and putting out their tiny little hands for nuts. Mrs. Patel gave the children a packet of nuts each, and they threw the nuts away from the Jeep so the monkeys jumped off after them. Some monkeys, the larger, older ones, sat on the side of the path, and whenever the children waved to them, they would wave back solemnly.

'It's a pity,' said Rohan, 'that not one of the peacocks has come to sit on the Jeep as they usually do.'

'Yes,' agreed his mother with a sigh, 'and much as I dislike them scrounging for worms in my tomato beds, I must say I miss them wandering freely in and out of the garden. And though I confess that they have the most raucous voices, I miss hearing them as often as we did before.'

'But what about Sunder and Sunderi?' asked Gina anxiously, naming the peacock and peahen who usually ran tame around their house. 'Has something happened to them, too?'

'No, of course not, darling,' said her mother quickly, 'but they seem to be very uneasy these days and stick close to the house and garden, not venturing far into the jungle any more. They don't dance as often as they did earlier, and we rarely see the other birds which used to roam the gardens and eat out of the birdhouses.'

'It's because of those horrible poachers,' said Anu angrily. 'But don't worry, Gina, once we catch them, the peacocks will feel safe again.'

'Yeah,' said Gina, cheering up.

They enjoyed the rest of the ride and soon the Jeep drove into their driveway.

'Home at last! Yay!' squealed Gina excitedly.

It was 1 p.m. and Mr. Patel was not due back home for a few hours yet. The Patels tumbled out with Hunter, and a couple of men came to greet them and help with their luggage.

'Ashok! Vijay!' said Nimal greeting the two men who had been with the Conservation for over ten years. 'This is Hunter, our new dog. Hunter, shake with friends.'

'What a smart dog,' said Ashok, as he and Vijay shook Hunter's paw. 'How did you get him?'

'May we tell you the story later?' asked Rohan.

'Sure thing,' said Vijay, 'we'll take your suitcases in. I know you're all dying to rush around the house and garden to see what's new, so go ahead. We can catch up on news later. No, don't worry,' he added with a grin as Rohan and Nimal turned to help, 'Ashok and I have been working out and can carry your luggage easily, without your assistance. Thanks, though.'

Gina asked eagerly, 'Where's Vida?'

'She's in the kitchen putting the finishing touches to a large meal for all of you,' said Ashok with a grin. 'She knew you would be "starving" as usual.'

Vida was Mrs. Patel's assistant, both with housework and administration of the Conservation, and Mrs. Patel often said she would never have been able to manage everything if not for Vida. Vida started out by being a helper to Mrs. Patel when Rohan was born, and had looked after all the children, including Nimal. However, Mrs. Patel had encouraged her to develop in other ways, and Vida had grown tremendously in her skills. She and Ashok were married a year ago.

The Patels rushed off to see Vida.

'Vida! Vida!' shrieked Gina as she tumbled into the kitchen ahead of the others and pounced on Vida, giving her a big hug.

'Help! I'm going to be smothered,' cried Vida as the others crowded into the large kitchen and surrounded her, all trying to hug her at once.

'My goodness – how you've all grown since I last saw you!' Vida exclaimed, hugging each of them in turn. 'Nimal, you're taller than Anu. How on earth did you manage it? I'm impressed.'

They laughed happily. It was grand to be home and meet everyone again. Hunter was introduced to Vida and she was most impressed with him and happy for the children.

'Off with you for now,' said Vida, shooing them out of the kitchen a little later. 'Go and check out everything and come to the dining room for lunch in half an hour. Yes, there's chocolate cake, Gina, so stop nosing around under the dish covers.'

Laughing at Vida, they trooped off, each rushing off to explore, on their own, their favourite haunts.

It was a massive house and had two floors. The ground floor had a humongous living and dining room which could seat at least 50 people with ease; a smaller dining room leading off the kitchen could seat a dozen or more, and they usually ate in there. The kitchen was large and there was also a big storage room with huge freezers and shelves on which frozen goods and other bulk items could be stocked, since the town was some distance away. There was an enormous study/library, with bookshelves lining three walls, floor to ceiling, and thousands of books on an eclectic selection of topics. Mr. Patel had a computer set up there, as well as a desk for his work. The room in which Mrs. Patel and her office crew operated was also located on the ground floor. There were eight bedrooms upstairs, and five bathrooms – three upstairs and two on the ground floor. The children also had their own library upstairs where two sides of the room were lined with tall bookshelves. Their parents had always encouraged them to read, collect and treat books with care, and all the children loved reading. Nice shady verandahs ran around the whole house, and there was big vegetable garden at the back with a good-sized flower garden in front.

A ten-minute walk away from the house was another building which housed an auditorium in which lectures to the public were held. This auditorium served the dual purpose of being used not only for lectures on conservation issues, but also as a theatre for cultural events. There were several other large rooms which were used for entertaining visitors, holding educational seminars and symposiums, and also for fundraising events. It was called the Durrell Auditorium.

The stores and cafeteria were in another building next to the auditorium and the tours started from the same area; there were a few rest houses which were spaced out to ensure privacy. The majority of the rest houses were located in the 'Conservationists' Heaven', and staffed by a greater number of people, some of whom were experienced trackers and rangers.

'Gosh,' said Nimal, as he met the others in the dining room fifteen minutes later, 'my parents have sent us tons of things in the trunk – I vote we check it out after lunch. I didn't delve into it, but it looks as if there's some interesting stuff. Hunter tried to pull out some odds and ends, but I closed the trunk.'

'Goody, goody!' exclaimed Gina, who loved surprises. 'Maybe we'll find things in it that we can take to our cave. You know what – there's a new rabbit hutch and six white rabbits in the back garden. They're really sweet.'

'I saw them, too,' said Nimal. 'I also managed to get the peacocks to come to me, though they were hiding in some thick bushes when I first went out.'

'Did you see the latest selection of books in the library?' asked Anu eagerly. 'There are at least ten on animals and birds, and then lots on other topics, as well. Boy – it would be great if Dad would let us borrow two or three to take down to our cave.'

'There's also a new bookshelf in *our* library,' she continued. 'Maybe we can fill it up over the next year.'

'I know my parents have sent us some books, too,' said Nimal.

'They always do,' commented Rohan, 'No, Anu, don't disappear just this minute to check them out. It's two minutes to lunch time and you know Mum likes us to be punctual.' He smiled at Anu's mock grimace and continued, 'Did any of you see the clearing on the west side of the house?'

'No, I didn't,' said Nimal.

The girls hadn't noticed it either.

'You'll never guess what it's for,' said Rohan in a tone of suppressed excitement. 'I couldn't believe it when I asked one of the men who was working on it and he told me.'

'Rohan,' threatened Anu as she, Nimal and Gina all advanced on him menacingly. 'Hurry up and tell us before we tickle you to death.'

'We're not part of one of your suspense or mystery books,' added Nimal, 'out with the secret.'

'Well,' said Rohan, backing away and dragging it out till he bumped into the wall, 'it's the site for a real, concrete, swimming pool.'

'Yippee!' yelled the others joyfully.

'Oh, we've wanted one for years and years,' said Nimal, 'and now, finally, our dream's coming true. I loved our muddy swimming pool,' he added, referring to the pool at the back of the house. 'At least we all learned how to swim in it so we were okay at school, but a real pool – wow!'

'When will it be ready?' asked Gina eagerly. 'Next week?'

She had been swimming since she was tiny. She had absolutely no fear in the water and, along with Nimal, was an excellent swimmer. As Rohan often said, 'She's like a fish in the water and swims underwater, too'.

'No, of course not,' said Rohan with a laugh, 'they only got the okay last week, and have just started on the clearing. They said it would be ready by November.'

'But that's too late for this year,' wailed Gina disappointedly.

'Yeah, I know, but pools take a long time to build. It'll be a really large pool – I saw the plan – and there'll be diving boards, too.'

'How will they keep birds and animals from using it as a watering hole?' asked Nimal with a grin.

'Well, it's going to be a closed and covered pool, and if we can afford it next year, it may even be heated so that it can be used in the winter as well,' replied Rohan. 'Also, the tourists will be able to use it and it'll be an added attraction.'

'Aren't we lucky?' said Anu. 'All these wonderful things we have, and can do, at home. I wish our school were here, too, so that we never had to go away. It would be pure bliss.' She often struggled between being an extrovert and an introvert.

The others chuckled at her dreamy expression.

'Ah, there you are,' said Vida, coming into the room with a loaded tray. 'Thank you, Rohan,' she added as he immediately went over to take the tray from her. 'Just put it down on the table, and the rest of you lay out the food. There's another tray to come.'

'I'll get it for you, Vida,' offered Nimal, as he tripped over Hunter and stumbled towards the door.

'No thanks, Nimal,' said Vida laughing. 'Knowing you – and I see that you haven't changed all that much – you'd probably catch your feet in some air and drop all the food. Let Rohan get it and you help here.'

'Well – I'm hurt beyond words,' moaned Nimal, as he tried unsuccessfully to put on a sorrowful face. 'Me trip over nothing? Are you actually calling me clumsy, Vida?'

'Get along with you,' said Vida with a grin as she moved between the kitchen and the dining room. 'You know you're a Grade A klutz, Nimal. But maybe – one day – you'll improve.'

'I get insulted the minute I get home,' muttered Nimal. 'Oh, well, I guess I'll just have to hug you for that, Vida.'

He gave her a quick hug and nearly knocked over the large dish of chicken curry she was holding. 'Oops! I guess I am better off holding the door open for Rohan.'

'Oooh! Chocolate cake!' said Gina hungrily, as Rohan brought in another tray of food. 'What a feast! Let's start eating, quick.'

'We must wait for your mum and the others,' said Vida. 'They'll be here soon. Why don't you all sit down till then?'

'My family – all together again,' said their mother, walking in a couple of minutes later. 'Do you think you can hold off eating for ten more minutes without starving?'

'I don't know about Gina,' said Rohan, pointing at the little girl who had a finger in her mouth. 'She's already chewing on her fingers.'

'No, I'm not,' said Gina indignantly. 'I was just licking off a bit of the icing from the cake. Of course I can wait, Mum, but why?'

'I just got a call from your father,' said Mrs. Patel, 'and he said he'd be able to join us for lunch and go back to work later.'

'Great!' said Rohan. 'Then we can hear all the latest news about the peacocks.'

'It's a really bad state of affairs,' said Mrs. Patel. 'Your dad will give you all the gory details.'

Ashok and Vijay came in a few minutes later and then Mr. Patel arrived. The children rushed to greet him and, of course, Hunter had to be introduced.

'He is a fine dog,' said Mr. Patel, stroking Hunter who sat at his feet with his tongue hanging out. 'How did you get him?'

'Well, now that everyone's here, maybe Anu can tell you the story,' said Rohan.

'It all began like this,' said Anu, and she told them the story as they ate a delicious meal of rice, rotis, curries cooked in exotic spices, and washed it down with lime juice and water.

They enjoyed the story and chuckled when they heard about some of Hunter's strange habits and of the way in which he had greeted Mrs. Patel.

'That's just incredible,' said Ashok at the end of the tale. 'I would love to see him eat a grape. Do we have any grapes in the house, Vida?'

'Yes, I'll get a few,' said Vida getting up and going to the fridge in the kitchen.

She came back with a handful of grapes, and everyone watched in amazement as Hunter went through his routine. He didn't seem to be bothered by the fact that he was being stared at while he was eating; and he finished up the grapes and waited, hopefully, for more food. He had been given his own bowl with lots of goodies in it, and he was wishing he could have a piece of the chocolate cake his nose told him was on the table.

'Smart dog that,' said Mr. Patel. 'Well, does anyone want to tell me how they did at school, or is Hunter the camouflage for bad marks?'

Smiling in negation of his teasing accusation, the children told him how they had fared.

'Good work, all of you,' said Mr. Patel, 'I am so glad you each did well at something. Gina, I want to hear your limerick, and maybe if we all think it's good, you can have an extra big piece of cake.'

While Mrs. Patel and Vida handed out plates with huge slices of cake, Gina sang her limerick, was applauded loudly, and claimed a large piece of cake. She was very pleased with herself. Hunter also got a piece of cake.

'All done?' asked Mrs. Patel at last.

'Yes, thanks. I couldn't eat another thing,' said Nimal.

'Good – then I won't have to make you supper,' teased his aunt, as the men cleared the table, and she and Vida poured out tea for the adults and milk for the children and Hunter.

Nimal looked alarmed. 'But,' he began, and then saw the twinkle in Mrs. Patel's eyes and grinned as he said, 'I may last without food for an hour or so, Aunty, but – I'll be back! You know, I really miss home cooking – the food at school is good, but they can never make a chicken curry or dhal like we get at home.'

Just then a beautiful peacock walked into the room, the peahen trailing behind him.

'Sunder and Sunderi!' exclaimed Nimal, promptly getting up from his seat.

He knelt on the floor and the birds came right up to him, fearlessly accepting bits of food. The others crowded around them.

'Gosh, can you imagine anyone wanting to hurt such gorgeous creatures?' asked Anu, as they all stroked the birds.

Hunter came up curiously to see what all the fuss was about, and the birds stared him right in the eye, equally curious as to what kind of a creature he was.

Nimal made Hunter sit beside him and then said, in the special tones he used for animals, 'Hunter, these are friends.' He put an arm around each of the birds who, quite unafraid of anything as long as Nimal was with them, stayed still.

Hunter sniffed at them and then, giving a small whine, went closer to the birds. They did not back away, and after a few seconds of mutual staring, Hunter lay down. Sunder – who was the peacock – looked at the dog for a moment and then went and sat down on one side of him. Sunderi, the peahen, followed her mate's example and sat down on the other side. A few minutes later they were all asleep, as if they had known each other for years.

'Well, just look at that!' exclaimed Mr. Patel in wonder. 'Now, if only human beings could get along as well.'

'Amazing dog, that,' said Ashok, and everyone agreed.

'Guess what?' said Anu as they settled back around the table. 'We've decided to form a group called the "JEACs".'

'Oh? And what does that acronym stand for?' inquired Mr. Patel.

'Junior Environmentalists and Conservationists,' said Anu.

They explained further and the adults were very pleased to see the children taking the initiative in starting such a group.

'Good for you,' said Mrs. Patel, beaming around the table. 'Let me know when you want to discuss details and I'll be happy to help in any way possible.'

'Thanks a ton,' chorused the JEACs.

'What's new on the Conservation, Dad?' asked Anu. 'Any other plans – other than the swimming pool, which we've heard about?'

'Well, a couple of things,' said Mr. Patel. 'You must have heard that the Nawab of Patankot died last month, right?' As the children nodded, he continued, 'In his will, he left us a large sum of money to be used to improve the Conservation – if you remember, he was an avid conservationist.'

'Wow! So how will you use it, Uncle Jim?' asked Nimal eagerly. 'Was it a very large sum?'

'Extremely generous,' said Mr. Patel. 'We have enough to put into effect two plans we've been thinking of for a long time – the petting zoo, and a small railway line. Naturally they will be named after the Nawab and his wife.'

'Superfab!' said Anu excitedly. 'How long will it take to set these up, Dad?'

'They should be ready by next year,' said Mr. Patel. He held up his hands, laughing as the children showered him with questions. 'Whoa! One at a time. The library has a detailed plan of the route the railway line will take.'

'Will all the animals for the zoo be taken from our Conservation?' asked Nimal.

'No, we'll have to buy some, but that won't cost a lot,' said Mr. Patel. 'The government is clearing away part of the Shalimar Conservation, and there are many animals which can be relocated to us – and the government will pay for it as they want to avoid too much negative publicity. That's being done in March next year, and there should be plenty of young ones for us to put in our petting zoo.'

'Oh, Dad,' said Anu, 'doesn't that mean that even more people with small kids will come to the Conservation so that they can take their children to a zoo?'

'It sure does, Anu,' said Mr. Patel. 'And the train ride will be a big attraction – a trip to waterholes without them having to carry their kids. We may raise funds to put up a small Kiddies' Park, too. The sooner children are introduced to animals and learn to love them, the better for conservation.

'The problem with the peacocks, though,' he continued, 'is really worrying.'

'Yeah, Dad,' said Rohan, 'we met Peter on the train and he told us about the poachers killing the peacocks. Could you give us more details, please?' He told his father what they already knew.

'I have a few more details,' said Mr. Patel soberly. 'We found the carcasses of ten peacocks, and after doing an approximate count of the live birds, discovered that twenty more were missing. You can imagine how angry we were. All of us have spent many sleepless nights trying to catch the crooks.'

The children listened in silence, as Mr. Patel continued grimly.

'Then, a week ago, at the small waterhole near the gates, when Haren was patrolling that area, he heard a gunshot close by. He called the others on his mobile as he ran towards the sound. Bill was closest to him and caught up with him quickly. They set off towards the area from which the shot had been heard. All of a sudden, Haren saw two men running away from the bushes where they had obviously been hiding. He yelled to them to stop – that he had a gun – but of course they didn't listen to him.

'In the dark, despite powerful torches, Bill and Haren lost sight of the men. They could not even hear footsteps. But they felt the chaps must be close by, so they searched each bush in the area carefully.

'In the meantime, the rest of us were making tracks to that spot as fast as possible – we had heard the shots and shouting. The poachers must have realized they would have to make a run for it before more men arrived because, just as Bill saw a flash of metal behind a large bush he was approaching, there was another gunshot. Down went poor Bill – with a bullet in his leg. He yelled to Haren, who rushed to the place, but the men were desperate to get away and they shot Haren, too – in the thigh. Bill tried to get a shot at them but could not reach his gun, which he had dropped when he went down.

'The poachers dashed off leaving the peacock, feathers and all. By the time we arrived on the scene, ten minutes later, there was no sign of the crooks – they had a good head start. We knew it would be futile to go after them, and in any case, Bill and Haren were bleeding badly. So, three men went off to see if they could discover any trace of the poachers, and the rest of us attended to Bill and Haren.'

The children were appalled.

'How are they now?' asked Anu anxiously, 'I mean Bill and Haren, of course.'

'They had to be hospitalized, both of them,' said Mr. Patel. 'Bill injured his right shin, and had to undergo immediate surgery. He's now in a cast and can't walk for a month. He wanted to stay here, but I sent him home for a couple of weeks so that he could get complete rest, and we keep in touch daily. He wants to come back soon though.'

'What about Haren?' asked Rohan. 'Did he also have to go home?'

'No, he's back from the hospital and in his room. He only got a flesh wound, but they had to remove the bullet and he was given twenty stitches in his thigh. He'll be unable to walk for a couple of weeks, and after that he'll have to go slow for a while. But he can help with feeding the baby animals and doing odd jobs around the menagerie, which will give Ben some time to catch up on his writing.'

Ben DeSouza was one of the vets who looked after the menagerie of injured and baby animals. He also wrote articles for veterinary magazines.

He and his wife shared a large house with the other vet Mano Goswami, Bill and Haren.

'Those men are terrible,' cried Gina. 'How could they shoot Haren and Bill, and kill our beautiful birds?'

The little girl was crying with anger, and Mr. Patel gave her a hug.

'Well, honey,' he said soothingly, 'they're nasty, greedy men. But now that Peter's on the case, I am sure we'll catch them before they do much more harm.'

'Dad, Peter said we could help him by keeping an eye on things from our cave, and by wandering around the waterholes in pairs or a group,' said Rohan. 'We think we may find some clues. Has anyone got an idea as to how the poachers enter the Conservation?'

'We suspect they have a hideout in the Conservation itself,' said Ashok. 'They never seem to leave any footprints around the wall, nor many clues.'

'However, we did find a round mark in some wet soil at a waterhole,' said Mr. Patel.

'Do you know how the mark was made?' queried Rohan.

'We're not quite sure,' said Vijay slowly, 'but Mike thought it might be from a bag which was used to put the feathers into.'

'Where was this?' asked Nimal eagerly.

'At the waterhole where Haren and Bill were shot,' said Ashok.

'But we've posted men there, three nights in a row, and have not seen any trace of those crooks,' said Mr. Patel wearily. 'And then we hear shots in some other area of the jungle. It's extremely frustrating, to say the least. Also, everyone has so much other work that it's impossible to keep an eye on all the waterholes every night. We even seconded some of the staff from CH, but have had no luck.'

'But how on earth did they get in?' asked Anu. 'It's impossible to climb any of the walls as they're so high and they'd be electrocuted by the fence on it; and there's only one entrance which no one can get through unless the chowkidar lets them in. Do you think they're hiding out in the CH?'

'We don't think so, Anu,' said Ashok, 'since we believe it would be too dangerous for them to wander around there without trained escorts – the larger wildlife would be too dangerous for anyone who doesn't know how to avoid trouble. It's easier, and safer, for them to hide out in the HP. It's a terrible situation that has us flummoxed.'

'Ashok's right and I think you children can definitely help if you stay in your cave for a few days,' said Mr. Patel. 'Pete's idea is a good one. Keep in mind, these crooks are extremely dangerous and won't hesitate to harm you, though I doubt they will shoot at you. Be very, very careful, please. Your cave is quite safe. It does overlook the largest waterhole and, as you know, the peacocks visit it frequently. Also, with Hunter around, he can warn you of any danger.'

'Thanks, Dad,' said Rohan, relieved to hear his father agree to them being in on the case. 'We'll take care.'

'Good luck, then,' said Mr. Patel who knew they would not do anything foolish. 'I guess I had better get back to work now. I'll be back home really late, Dilki,' he continued, turning to his wife, 'probably around midnight. I need to discuss some matters with the staff at CH. I'll get something to eat when I get in, so don't wait up for me. Nimal, say hello to your parents and tell your father that the gate is working well. I'll call him on his mobile phone when I have a few minutes. Goodbye, kids – it's nice to have you home – I'll see you all sometime tomorrow, I guess.'

'Well, Dad,' said Rohan, 'we may go to the cave tomorrow afternoon.'

'Okay, I'll try and make breakfast, and look out for one of you to leave messages for us near the waterhole each day, so that we know you're safe. Our usual signals of a couple of scratches on the big tree opposite your cave will be fine – you know the codes.'

'Sure thing, Dad,' said Rohan, 'you can count on us – can't he, JEACs?'

The others nodded their heads vigorously, and Hunter barked in agreement.

'Dad, when will we see Mike?' asked Gina.

'He's really busy today, and is sorry he can't come over this evening – he has to deal with an emergency at the CH. But he sent his love and said he'd meet you tomorrow at Peter's place,' said Mr. Patel.

Mike Carpenter was a favourite with the Patels, and Peter's best friend. Assistant Manager of the Conservation and Mr. Patel's right-hand man, he spent his time between HP and CH. He lived with the Mallicks, another young couple who lived and worked on the Conservation.

'Goodo!' said the youngsters.

'Dad,' said Anu, 'have you heard from Uncle Jack recently?'

Jack Larkin was an Australian, and a good friend of Mr. and Mrs. Patel's. Mr. Patel and Mr. Larkin had met many years ago at an international conference on conservation. The children adored 'Uncle Jack', as they called him.

'Yes, I spoke to him yesterday,' replied her father. 'He's very busy just now with some new plans he has for a conservation in Brisbane, in the Gold Coast area. But he said he would be in touch later on – I don't know too many details at the moment.'

'Oh, too bad,' said Nimal. 'That means that we won't see him this summer at all.'

'I'm sure he'll survive,' said Mr. Patel with a smile. 'Now, I really have to run. See you later, folks.'

They waved goodbye to Mr. Patel, and also to Ashok and Vijay who were accompanying him.

Everyone else helped to clear the table and load up the dishwashers.

CHAPTER 6

A Trunk Full of Surprises

'Aunty, do you mind if we go up and see what my parents sent us?' asked Nimal, once all the chores were done.

'Of course not, Nimal,' said Mrs. Patel. 'Why don't you take the trunk to your library – there is more room for all of you there.'

'Good idea, Mum,' said Rohan. 'We'll see you later.'

They thanked Vida for the fabulous meal she had prepared for them and hurried upstairs.

The trunk was very big and extremely heavy. However, the boys were quite muscular and easily managed to carry it to their library. They put it in the middle of the room and everyone, including Hunter, crowded around eagerly as Nimal opened it up.

'Oooh! Books! Lots of them,' cried Anu in delight, as she discovered a layer of books right on top.

'All our favourites, too,' said Rohan, pulling out the Sherlock Holmes and P.G. Wodehouse books, obviously meant for him.

'A Gerald Durrell and a Herriot book for me,' exclaimed Nimal, taking them out, 'and Harry Potter and Susan Cooper books for you, Anu.'

'Nesbit books for me, and some Enid Blyton,' cried Gina taking out her share.

'And more *Asterix* for all of us,' said Anu. 'Oh, do let's put them on our new shelves now – I can't bear to see empty bookshelves.'

'Let's take some of these to the cave,' suggested Rohan. 'We'll need some books to read while we're there.'

'But of course – that's a great idea,' said Anu, who always had at least three books on the go. 'Maybe we can borrow a couple of bright lanterns from Mum and cover the opening from the cave so that the light can't be seen.'

'No need to borrow anything,' said Nimal, who was rummaging in the trunk. 'Look, we have two little lanterns of our own.' He showed them the lanterns saying, 'They're safe to use, and you don't even need matches to light them. You just turn the knob and – *voilà*! They light up. They're perfect.' He demonstrated how the lanterns worked and the others were equally delighted with them.

'What are these green and brown clothes?' asked Gina, as she tugged one garment out of the trunk.

The others looked at it in surprise. They pulled out more of the clothes and found four sets of pants, shirts, socks and caps, all in shades of dark green and brown; one set for each child.

'I know why they're that colour,' said Rohan suddenly. The others looked at him expectantly. 'It's for camouflage. If we wear these in the jungle it'll be extremely difficult for anyone to see us because we'll meld in with the colours of the jungle.'

'Of course – you've hit the nail on the head, or rather, *Rem acu tetigisti*, as Bertie Wooster would say,' exclaimed Nimal, who had recently been reading the 'Jeeves' books by P.G. Wodehouse, and enjoyed using some of the Latin and French expressions in them. 'These are great. I guess the APs put them in for fun since we wander around the jungle so much, but these clothes will really be useful when we're trying to catch the crooks.'

'What else is there?' asked Anu.

'Pots, pans and a little stove, also for our cave,' came Gina's voice, muffled because she had her head in the trunk. She pulled out the things and passed them to Anu.

'Your parents must have known we were planning to get all kinds of things for our cave, since we spend so much time in it,' said Anu. 'How thoughtful of them – there's even a good-sized cooler, and a large, inflatable water carrier.'

'And tons of canned food,' said Rohan. 'Turkey, cheese, biscuits, peaches, pineapple, mangoes, ham, luncheon meat, tuna, corn and meat balls.'

'Oooh, stop! Do put a sock in it, yaar,' groaned Nimal. 'I'm beginning to feel hungry again.'

The others giggled, as Rohan continued, 'There's loads of other stuff, too – no wonder the trunk weighed a ton.'

'There's even a set of plastic plates, mugs and cutlery, and a can opener,' said Nimal. 'We won't need to buy a thing for the cave.'

'And more books at the bottom of the trunk,' said Anu happily.

She and Gina fished out the books.

'Oh, what a beaut!' cried Nimal, as he was handed a large book by the famous writer Simon Barnes, titled *Planet Zoo*. 'I must take this to the cave.'

'And a massive book about detectives and true cases they have solved, and also a beautiful book on birds and animals in North America,' said Rohan delightedly.

'Here's a book of limericks and poems for you, Gina,' said Anu handing it over, 'and a book on writing for me; and lots of note books for my stories.'

'Wow! Look at these fabulous books on sea and river creatures and their habits. You can't get these books in India, Nimal, so your parents must have picked them up when they were in England,' said Rohan, as he emptied the trunk. 'Man – are we ever lucky your parents travel around a lot and always send us useful and fun things.'

'Well, we must thank them over the phone tonight,' said Anu, 'and maybe we can each make them something as a thank you gift.'

'Good idea,' said Rohan. 'Gina, call Mum so that she can see what we got, while Nimal and I take the trunk to the storage room.'

'Okay,' said Gina, and ran off to find her mother.

'I'll sort out what we want for the cave,' said Anu.

The boys went off with the trunk and returned just as Gina and Mrs. Patel entered the library.

'My goodness me! You certainly are fortunate children,' said Mrs. Patel with a smile, as she admired everything on the floor. 'You'll need some help getting it all to your cave tomorrow. Maybe Ashok and Vijay can take a couple of hours off.'

'Thanks, Mum, that's a brainwave,' said Rohan, giving her a quick hug. 'If we put a lot of the things in sacks, along with our sleeping bags, and the smaller items in our knapsacks, we should be fine.'

'Sounds like a good plan, son. Now, I need to go and do a bit of work. You know there's that big fundraiser in Hardwar in a few days – twenty volunteers are coming over in half an hour, and I need to get them started on some of the administrative work that needs to get done,' said Mrs. Patel. 'By the way, I assume that you kids will not be attending this particular fundraiser, right?'

'Do you mind, Mum?' asked Anu apologetically.

'Of course not – catching the crooks is more important just now, where you folk are concerned. As you know, there are always plenty of fundraisers for you to help out with, and attend, later on,' said Mrs. Patel understandingly. 'Perhaps the JEACs can also do a fundraiser at some point in time.'

'Thanks, Mum, thanks, Aunty,' chorused the children gratefully.

'We'd love to do a JEACs' fundraiser, Mum,' said Anu. 'Also, Mum, since we have so much, I thought we could sort out gently used clothes, toys and other items, and give them to our church. In your last email you mentioned that one of your groups was collecting things for a community that had very little, and there were many children between the ages of six and sixteen.'

'Excellent idea, honey,' said Mrs. Patel. 'We need things by the end of this month, and any donation will be greatly appreciated.'

'Brilliant, sis; I'll also give some of my pocket money to purchase new items,' offered Rohan.

'So will I,' chorused the other three, and Mrs. Patel nodded in a satisfied way. All four parents tried to lead by example, and the children were caring and generous; they were always willing to share whatever they had.

'Now, remember, dinner will be at 7 p.m. and your parents will call around ten, Nimal,' concluded Mrs. Patel.

'We'll be there, Aunty,' said Nimal. 'You can't possibly imagine I would be late for a meal, now could you? Oh, would you wait a second, please? I have something for you.'

He ran off to his room and returned to give her one of the carved boxes he had picked up.

'I hope you like it, Aunty Dilki,' said Nimal, handing it over. 'I got one for the mater, too – with different carvings.'

'Nimal, this is beautiful!' exclaimed Mrs. Patel, turning the box around to admire the carvings. 'Thank you, so much,' she said, hugging the boy. 'I will put some of my good jewellery in it.'

She went off, and the children made a list of all the things they would need, and drew up a tentative plan of action which they could run past Peter in the morning.

They worked hard for a few hours, only breaking off for a quick 'self-served' tea, since Mrs. Patel and Vida were both busy with the volunteers.

'I think we're in pretty good shape now,' said Rohan, putting down his pen, and closing his notebook. 'Let's put the things we need in the sacks now, since we've got a bit of time before dinner. Nimal, could you and Gina find the sleeping bags and bring them here? I'll get some strong sacks, and Anu, get some food from Vida – not that we don't have tons of things here, but after all, we *are* growing kids.'

'Aye, aye, Captain,' said Nimal, saluting smartly.

They dashed off in different directions. Rohan was back first, with the sacks, and he went to his room to get the umbrella out of his suitcase. He covered the second button with tape and put the umbrella at the bottom of one of the sacks; then he commenced filling up the sack with clothes and pots and pans.

The others arrived and everything was piled into the sacks. The water carrier was filled, and the vegetables and eggs were put in the cooler.

'Well, we've finished just in time to wash and go down for dinner,' said Anu, putting the last item in the sack.

'Four large sacks,' said Rohan. 'Nimal and I can each carry one, as well as our knapsacks, and Ashok and Vijay can take a sack each. If you girls can carry your knapsacks, the water carrier and cooler, we should be able to manage it all in one trip.'

'No problemo,' said Anu.

'Good thinking, yaar,' said Nimal. 'Now, let's go and wash. I'm starved!' He led the way out of the library, ignoring the rude laughter that followed him.

'Good, you're just in time,' said Vida, looking up from the turkey she was slicing at the table. 'Rohan, could you bring in the tray from the kitchen, and Anu, please pour out juice for everyone.'

'Mmmm, turkey dinner and all the fixings – even cranberry sauce,' said Nimal, sniffing eagerly. 'I do love the cosmopolitan mixture of food you give us, Vida. Jacob says that we're world citizens where literature is concerned, and I would add that we're also world citizens where food is concerned.'

'I'm glad to hear that,' said Vida, who loved trying out new recipes from all over the world.

Mrs. Patel joined them and they had a fun time at the meal, telling Mrs. Patel and Vida about all the things that happened in school.

'And did you play any more tricks on the boys, Nimal?' asked Vida, who loved to hear about the crazy tricks Nimal got up to in school.

'Actually, just one, this term,' said Nimal with a grin.

'Oh, do tell us,' begged Gina.

'Okay,' said Nimal obligingly. 'You know I've told you about this pompous chap in my class – Mohan – who thinks he's the cat's whiskers just because his parents are very rich? Well, he always puts on airs, especially when he's playing cricket. He thinks he's the top bowler in the universe, and loves to boast of how he bowled maiden overs the last time he played against a team at home, blah, blah, blah.'

'What's a maiden over?' asked Gina who was only just beginning to follow cricket and was learning the proper terminology.

'Well, you know that there are six balls in an over, right?' explained Rohan, patiently. Gina nodded and he continued, 'If you bowl all six, and not a single run is scored, it's called a "maiden over".'

'Thanks, Rohan,' said Gina. 'So what happened next, Nimal?'

'Of course, he never bowls maiden overs while at school,' continued Nimal. 'Anyway, a number of us were getting pretty fed up with all his big talk. I racked my brains as to how we could make him shut up about his maiden overs. And then I had a brainwave! I went into town and bought what I needed.' He looked at the expectant faces around the table and paused.

'And then what did you do? Hurry up, Nimal,' said Anu.

Nimal grinned cheekily and continued. 'The next week we were all asked to practise at the nets. Of course Mohan felt he didn't need much practice, but said he would come out for ten minutes when we had all finished, just to show us poor chaps how to *really* bowl. The situation was ideal and with the help of Rohan and a few others, I set the scene for Mohan. Rohan was going to face Mohan's bowling and I would be the wicket keeper. We had just got everything ready when Mohan arrived. He had brought along some of his sycophants who loved his purse more than him. It was perfect! Sorry, Gina – *sycophants* are people who suck up to others and flatter them without really meaning what they say.

'Well, Mohan swaggered over, rolled up his sleeves and waved an arm arrogantly for the ball. I tossed it to him. He measured out his pace and began his run.

'Rohan put his bat to the first three balls quite easily, much to Mohan's annoyance. I called out to him and said, "Come on, yaar, for goodness' sake, can't you bowl a maiden over? Rohan scored six runs off those balls." Needless to say, he didn't like that; he gave me a snooty look, and went even further back for his next ball. He started his run. I quickly removed the rubber band from the inflatable doll hidden behind the wickets – those dolls are simply amazing; they fold up flat and are held like that by a rubber band; the second you remove the rubber band, the doll inflates, in a jiffy, into a three-foot high girl. Mohan didn't even notice the doll since Rohan was blocking the wicket, but bowled to Rohan. Rohan stepped out of the way and deliberately let the ball hit the wickets and the doll was knocked down.

'Poor Mohan – he suddenly saw the doll lying on the ground behind the wickets and his face was a sight to behold. We hooted at him and rolled on the ground, roaring with laughter. "Oy, Mohan – that was some maiden you bowled over," yelled Rohan, and of course that set everyone off again. Mohan rushed off the field, his face a brilliant red because everyone was laughing at him, even his fans. We teased him mercilessly, and since that day we haven't heard any more talk about maiden overs bowled by him.'

'Oh, that's hilarious, Nimal. You're totally incorrigible,' cried Vida, wiping away tears of laughter. 'What happened to the maiden? I would love to see her.'

'I loaned her to a chap who wanted to play the trick on his older brother,' said Nimal, 'but I'll have it at Christmas time and you can see it then.'

They caught up on other news as they lazed around the table, laughing when Hunter wandered in from the kitchen, closely followed by Sunder and Sunderi, who appeared to have adopted the dog, and before they realized it, the telephone rang – it was 10 p.m.

'Nimal, please answer it – I'm sure it must be your parents. Use the library phone,' said Mrs. Patel, looking at her watch.

Nimal dashed off to the library. The others let him talk with his parents for a while, and then, when he called them, they each took turns to speak to their uncle and aunt, thanking them for the lovely gifts and telling them about their school term. Nimal had already told them about Hunter.

After the call, they were shooed off to bed.

'I know, I know. It's the first day you're home and you're too excited to sleep,' said Mrs. Patel as they protested that it was too early. 'But if you don't rest tonight, you will never get up in time to meet Peter at 7 tomorrow morning. Why don't you read a bit in bed?'

'Great idea, Mum,' said Anu. 'It's good to be home again and so nice to see you all,' she continued, giving her mother and Vida hugs and goodnight kisses.

'It's good to have you all back, too,' said Mrs. Patel as she kissed each of them goodnight and patted Hunter, who licked her hand. 'Shall I wake you up at 6 a.m. or do you have your alarm clocks?'

'I'll set mine, thanks, Mum,' said Rohan, 'and I'll wake the others.'

They trooped upstairs to their rooms. Rohan and Nimal each had their own room, and Hunter, of course, went with Nimal. Anu and Gina shared a room as the little girl was nervous of being on her own, and Anu did not mind sharing with her. However, Anu had a tiny corner which was sectioned off as her own little spot for 'retiring', as she called it, and she had a comfortable chair and desk in that area.

None of them, except for Anu, who 'retired' to her corner, read for too long. Anu was beginning to struggle, within herself, for space; and although she was as much of an extrovert as the others most of the time, she was finding, increasingly, that she needed time for herself and her writing. The struggle sometimes resulted in her withdrawing into herself – which some of her classmates called moody. Fortunately for her, her good friends, the boys, Gina and the rest of her family understood, and left her alone at these times.

Despite the excitement and anticipation of meeting Peter and Mike, and then going to their cave the next day, the children slept soundly till morning.

CHAPTER 7

What Haren Saw

'Anu! Anu! Wake up! It's 6 o'clock,' said Rohan, shaking her gently.

'Okay, I'm up,' said Anu, sitting up with a jerk. 'I'll get Gina and you try and wake Nimal – though that'll be like attempting to wake up the dead.'

'I'll get Hunter to wash his face for him,' said Rohan with a grin. 'I don't know anyone else who can sleep as soundly, or as long, as he can.'

'Nimal, time to rise,' said Rohan, going into Nimal's room a minute later and shaking the boy.

Nimal grunted, turned over and burrowed under the sheets. Hunter got up and licked Rohan's hand in greeting.

'Wake up, Nimal,' said Rohan again. 'Hunter, go and wake him,' he said to the dog, pointing at Nimal.

Hunter looked at Rohan, his intelligent brown eyes gleaming; then he leapt on to the bed, went over near Nimal's head, pulled away the sheet with his teeth, and licked his face.

'Oooh! What a sticky, licky dog you are,' groaned Nimal, laughing as he tried to push Hunter away. 'I'm up, I'm up,' he grunted, rolling out of bed with a bump.

'Well, you certainly haven't yet learned how to get out of bed rather than fall out of it,' said Rohan with a grin. 'Hurry, it's nearly 6:10 and we must be ready by 6:35 at the latest. You know it takes 25 minutes to get to Peter's place.'

'I'll be ready in a jiffy,' said Nimal. 'Go away and leave me in peace.'

'Don't go back to sleep,' teased Rohan, who knew Nimal would be ready in time. 'Next time I'll bring a bucket of water to help Hunter wake you up.'

He laughed, ducking out of the room as Nimal threw a pillow at him.

They dressed quickly and ran downstairs to greet Mrs. Patel, who had been up since 5 a.m. She told them that after meeting the CH staff, Mr. Patel had spent the night out in the jungle, trying to see if he could find out anything further about the poachers. He had then gone over to Peter's place to talk to him, and had spent the night there.

'Mrs. Collins just called me,' said Mrs. Patel, 'and offered to give all of you breakfast while you were chatting with Peter – so you had better hurry off as soon as possible.'

'I've poured out some juice,' said Vida, coming into the room with a tray full of glasses, 'and Hunter's already had a big bowl of milk and some biscuits.'

'Thanks, Vida – you're the greatest,' said Nimal, taking his glass and draining it so fast that he choked.

'Greedy chap,' said Rohan, slapping him on the back. 'Everyone ready? Okay – see you later, Mum, Vida.'

Waving goodbye to Mrs. Patel and Vida, the five set off for Peter's place, taking a bag of crumbs, some nuts and carrots, with which to feed the relatively tame birds, squirrels, monkeys and rabbits.

It was a beautiful morning. The sun was just rising, and they got brief glimpses of blue and pink sky through the trees; the dew was still fresh on the grass. They surprised a jackal with her cubs and stood still, as she called anxiously and shepherded the five little cubs away to her den. Though some of the birds came down and ate the crumbs the children held out, there was not one peacock to be seen. They threw nuts to the monkeys, who swung along in the trees above the children, chattering to them; and Nimal actually held a baby rabbit in his arms and fed it some carrot leaves.

Hunter came up and sniffed curiously at the bunny, which lay very still in Nimal's arms, staring at the dog with its bright eyes. As the others watched, quite enchanted, Nimal spoke softly both to Hunter and to the rabbit; Hunter sat down and putting out a paw tried, gently, to pat the bunny. The rabbit was quite unafraid – after all it was with Nimal – and it even tolerated Hunter sniffing at it. Nimal released the bunny, which darted off to join its family, and the youngsters moved along the path once more.

The walk ended all too soon, especially for Anu, who loved to dream along the way, drinking in the beauty and sounds of the jungle. They could hear an elephant trumpet somewhere in the distance, and even saw a herd of deer making their way down to a waterhole.

'Hello, everyone,' called Rohan as he opened the gate to Peter's home, and waved to Mr. and Mrs. Collins, Peter, Mike and Mr. Patel, who were seated on the verandah waiting for them.

The others went through the gates, which Rohan closed behind him, and greeted everyone. Hunter, of course, was fussed over by all the adults, and he just loved the attention.

Mike, a good-looking young man of 28, was six feet tall and very athletic – he also had a black belt in karate. He greeted the children affectionately and picked up Gina, who adored him, to seat her on his shoulders.

'Man, I sure missed all of you,' said Mike, beaming at them. 'And your dad just told us that you have a new name: the JEACs. Lots of excitement for you this summer, starting a new group and solving the problem of the peacocks for us. You're going to be busy.'

'Yes, we are,' chirruped Gina, tugging his hair gently and hugging him exuberantly. 'But we'll catch those crooks first, Mike.'

'Good,' said Mike, grinning at Peter. 'Pete, I think you have a great backup team here.'

'I know, I do,' said Peter.

'Now, before you start on case talk, let's eat,' said Mrs. Collins. 'I hope you are all hungry because I made a large breakfast and would hate it to be wasted.'

Hunter barked and looked up at her as if he had not eaten a square meal in a month.

'You hungry dog,' said Anu patting him. 'Aunty Nancy will think we're starving you. He's the only one who actually had something to eat before we left home this morning.'

'Well, I'm as hungry as Hunter,' said Nimal incorrigibly. 'Actually, even hungrier, and my mouth's watering because I know you make the *bestest* breakfasts in the whole world.'

'Flatterer,' said Mrs. Collins, who knew Nimal's capacity for food. 'Okay, who'll come and help me load the trays? I thought it would be nice to eat on the back verandah, since we have a wonderful view from there. Three of you will be enough – but not you, Nimal – I think you should keep Hunter and Mike company.'

Anu, Peter and Rohan went with her, while Nimal and Gina chatted with the others. The table was set and the food was soon dished out. Anu called the others when everything was ready, and they tucked into a good breakfast.

The adults wanted to know about school, and roared with laughter at Nimal's story about the 'maiden over'.

'What a smashing meal,' said Nimal, when he could not eat another thing. 'Thanks so much. One of the best things about the hols is that we get superb meals, not like at school. We starve during term time,' he added dolefully. 'Our cooks aren't half as good at making great meals as you, Aunty Dilki and Vida – could you give them some lessons?'

Everyone laughed. Nimal was notorious for complaining about the lack of good food in school, and nobody took him seriously. They knew he was on excellent terms with the school cooks, who were experts at catering for growing boys.

'Okay, now down to hard work,' said Peter. 'We've a lot of plans to make. As I was telling your father last night, I'm going to have to be based in Hardwar for the next few days. The case there is at a critical stage just now and I'm needed urgently. However, perhaps it also means that it'll be concluded rapidly, and I can move back here and give more time to this case. But at this stage, it's all up in the air, and I'll have to depend on you JEACs to do even more on your own. I can't come back here for two to three days. How do you feel about that?'

'No problemo,' said Rohan at once. 'I'm sure we'll be okay. Maybe we can even catch the crooks for you and wrap up this case – and Mike's here, too.'

'I doubt anything much will happen in three days, Pete,' said Mike. 'If these folks see the men or anything suspicious, they can come and tell one of us, and we'll deal with them.'

'When do you have to go back to Hardwar, Pete?' asked Nimal.

'Right away, unfortunately,' said Peter with a grimace. 'They want me to be there by noon today.'

'May we tell you about our ideas and plans, and then you can let us know if you think they're any good, and if they'll work?' asked Rohan eagerly. 'We had a brainstorming session last night.'

'Of course – go ahead, yaar,' said Peter.

'Well, our first step is to go over and see Haren, as soon as we've finished here,' said Rohan, consulting his notebook. 'We thought he may be able to give us even a brief description of the men, and what clothes they were wearing, in case we see any patches of clothing stuck on bushes; and then we may be able to find a trail and perhaps a few footprints.'

'Great idea,' said Mr. Patel. 'I'm impressed. All we thought of was that they were crooks, and we never realized that their clothing may lead us to more clues and, inevitably, to where they may be hiding.'

'Next, we thought the five of us could go down to the cave this evening,' said Rohan, 'just before dark. We'd pretend we were merely going to observe animals at the waterhole. We'll take all our gear down, with Ashok and Vijay's help, check to see if anyone's around and then hide it in the cave. Hunter would stand guard in the cave, while the four of us chat at the waterhole, in clear view of anyone who may be watching. Want to continue, Nimal?'

'Sure. Then, after some time, we would walk away, talking loudly about it being time to go home for supper. We'd go up the trail till we were behind the tree, out of sight of anyone at the waterhole, pretend to go on up the trail and then, noiselessly, double back and slip into our cave.'

'But how do you know that anyone will be watching you?' asked Mike, fascinated by the intricacy of their plans.

'Oh, we don't *know* that, Mike,' said Rohan. 'It's just a precaution.'

'What next?' asked Mr. Collins. He, too, was impressed by the detailed and careful planning they had done.

'We'll set up our things in the cave for the next few days,' said Anu. 'Once we're ready, we're going to change into our new clothes, which are perfect camouflage in the jungle. Rohan will take one walkie-talkie and go off to the waterhole on the west side of our cave, and Nimal, with the other handset, will go to the waterhole north of us. Gina, Hunter and I will stay in the cave so that we can keep an eye on things at the large waterhole which, as you know, is right in front of our cave. If there's any danger, we have Hunter to protect us. Gina and I will take turns to keep watch. Rohan and Nimal will listen for anything unusual, and check with each other to make sure they're all right.'

'How long are you planning to stay up each night?' asked Mrs. Collins in amazement.

'Some of us will be awake all night,' said Gina excitedly. 'We'll take turns to have a nap – both during the night and the day. After all, we never know when we'll see the crooks.'

'We'll also be snooping around the Conservation during the day,' said Rohan. 'It'll be easy enough, because the men won't suspect anything if they see four children with binoculars, and a dog, hanging around waterholes to observe the animals.'

'I have my sketch pad to draw any footprints,' said Nimal, 'and Anu has her camera, so when you need proof for a court case, hopefully we'll have some for you.'

'You sound as if you're all set to solve the case,' said Mike, 'and I certainly wish you all the best.'

'So do I,' said Mr. Patel. 'We'll look for messages from you to make sure you are okay – I'll arrange for Gune or Mano to check each morning. If you are in *any* danger at all, please use the flares, so that we can locate you.'

'Of course, Dad,' said Rohan. 'We've already packed some into our sacks.' He turned to Peter eagerly, 'Pete, what do you think of our plans? Do you think they make sense? If we need to, we'll change our plans according to the situation.'

'Sounds just great to me,' said Peter, 'and I have to congratulate you on your eye for detail. You've covered a lot of angles and I can't see what other plans can be made at this stage. I'm sure you'll find some clues – you're a sharp-eyed group. What time will you set off this evening?'

'It takes at least an hour to get to the waterhole, when we take it easy – and we'll have to, since we have lots of things to carry. If we leave at 4 p.m., we'll get there in good time to see some of the animals come to the waterhole, and then, after half an hour, we can move away.'

'Excellent planning,' said Peter. 'Well, it's 9 o'clock, and I have to leave shortly. Don't do anything dangerous – those men are tough customers, and won't stop at much. I'll look forward to hearing how you've progressed, via email from your father or Mike, and further details from you when I return on Saturday. You've got three days. Say hello to Haren, and tell him I hope he recovers quickly. I'll see him on my return. Hopefully you'll get a description of the men from him.'

'I'll note down everything,' said Rohan.

'Great! I have to run,' said Peter. 'Good luck, JEACs, and I hope you have an exciting adventure.'

'Good luck to you, too, Peter,' said Rohan, and the others echoed him.

'I'll send out email messages to all the staff when I get home this evening,' said Mr. Patel, 'giving them a synopsis of your plans, so that they are aware of what's going on.'

'I can do that for you, Jim,' said Mr. Collins. 'I have some time before I leave for the auditorium.'

'Thanks, Ronald,' said Mr. Patel, gratefully. 'Okay, kids – I'll be seeing you – and take care, won't you?'

'And watch out for those crooks,' added Mike, 'they're vicious.'

'Don't worry, we'll be careful,' said Anu.

The children thanked Mrs. Collins, said goodbye to everyone, and set off for the DeSouzas' place, to meet Haren. They had some fruit for him, a couple of books and a few comedy movies. The DeSouzas lived half an hour's walking distance from Peter's place.

The accommodation for staff was spread out over the Conservation, so that they covered a wide range. Each staff member had a cellular telephone and a portable computer, so that they could communicate effectively with each other; walkie-talkies were also used since, sometimes, there was no signal for the mobile telephone, depending on the density of the jungle.

Upon reaching the DeSouzas' home, also located in the HP section, they naturally had to visit the menagerie first and greet all the animals. They met Mr. DeSouza, who was attempting to calm down a small mongoose. It had been in a fight with another mongoose but was too scared to let Mr. DeSouza catch it and tend to it, and it was running round and round in the cage, where it had been placed half an hour ago. When it was first caught, it had been too stunned to protest much, since it had a badly bitten and swollen leg.

Mr. DeSouza greeted them and fussed over Hunter before he said, 'Nimal, see if you can get this creature to quieten down a bit, please.'

Nimal went over to the cage, the others watching eagerly – his charm with any animal never ceased to amaze everyone. Sitting down beside the cage, he began to whistle a peculiar little tune; the mongoose stopped running and stood still for a few moments. Nimal didn't move a muscle but just kept on whistling; the mongoose came towards him and sniffed at the boy's fingers. Opening the cage door, very slowly, Nimal stroked the creature; the mongoose stayed still and then, as Nimal picked it up gently, it snuggled into his arms contentedly.

'It's quite incredible what you can do with animals, Nimal!' exclaimed Mr. DeSouza. 'When are you going to start working with me? I wish you would become a vet – you could still be a conservationist. Bring the creature over here, please.'

Nimal grinned as he went over with the mongoose, which showed no signs of wanting to leave the boy. Mr. DeSouza attended to the creature as it lay quiescent in Nimal's arms, while the boy stroked it and talked to it softly. They put it into a comfortable cage with lots of soft moss, and it settled down calmly.

'Thanks, Nimal,' said Mr. DeSouza. 'It would've taken me most of the morning to attend to this little chap if you hadn't shown up. So, what brings you here this early in the morning? I wasn't expecting to see all of you before this afternoon or evening.'

'We came to see Haren,' said Rohan. 'We heard he was injured by the poachers and wondered how he was and, also, if he had a description of the crooks.'

'Poor Haren,' said Mr. DeSouza. 'He's much better now, but it was a bad injury. Go on in and chat with him – he's on his own at the moment. Yvette is already at the auditorium, getting ready for the lecture, and the rest of us have other work to do.' Yvette was Mr. DeSouza's wife, and she was responsible for all events at the auditorium. He continued, 'There is just so much TV Haren can watch, though he's been helping me with the animals. He helped your mother a great deal with her latest mail campaign and with paper work for the fundraiser in Hardwar. But you know what he's like – much prefers to be outside in the jungle than cooped up indoors.'

They went inside the house, up to Haren's room, and knocked on the open door.

'Come in,' called Haren.

'How are you, Haren?' asked Rohan, peering into the room. 'Do you feel like a few visitors?'

'Hey – how are you guys? Come on in,' said Haren, smiling broadly. 'It's great to see you again, and,' he added, noticing Hunter, 'whom do you have here?'

Hunter was introduced, and Haren was very impressed by the dog; naturally, Hunter's story was told all over again.

'We heard what happened to you and Bill, Haren,' said Anu, 'and we thought you might like some fruit and things.'

'Thanks a ton,' said Haren, gratefully, 'that was thoughtful of you. Actually, I get very bored at times. There are only so many times I can feed the baby animals, and I think it's more of a problem for the DeSouzas to bring them up to me rather than do the feeding themselves. However, they're really nice about it all, and once I'm able to walk a bit, it won't be too bad. Also, your dad and Mike have been bringing me books and movies.'

'I'm sure Mum was really glad of your help with her fundraiser,' said Anu tactfully. 'Uncle Ben told us you had helped her and Aunty Yvette a lot.'

They chatted for a while, telling Haren about their term at school and the new group they were planning to start. Gina recited her limerick, and Haren chuckled over it and praised the little girl. Then Nimal told him about the trick they had played on Mohan, and Haren laughed till he cried when he heard the story.

'You lot certainly cheered me up,' he said, wiping his eyes. 'Wish I could have seen Mohan's face.'

'Haren,' asked Rohan a little later, 'did you get a glimpse of the poachers at all, or was it too dark? We're hoping to do a bit of sleuthing over the next couple of days, and a few clues would be useful.'

'Unfortunately, it was too dark to see much,' said Haren, frowning angrily. 'That was one of the reasons we lost them so fast.'

'Oh – that's too bad,' said Rohan in disappointment. 'We hoped you might have noticed something, even a bit of their clothing.'

'Wait a second!' exclaimed Haren, staring into space, his eyes half closed as he tried to recall something.

The youngsters held their breath.

'I do remember seeing a red scarf,' said Haren slowly. 'I think it must have been when I first saw them emerge from the bushes and my torch picked up one chap. Yes,' he said excitedly, 'now that I think of it, I'm *positive* I saw a red scarf.'

He looked at them eagerly, 'Do you think that'll help you at all?' he asked.

'It's a beginning – the first real clue we have,' said Nimal.

'Well, good luck with your hunt,' said Haren. 'Those chaps make me really mad, and I sure wish I could go with you to capture them.'

They stayed with Haren for a while longer and then said goodbye – their visit had cheered him up considerably. It would take them an hour to get home, and they wanted to get a bit of sleep in the afternoon so that they could stay up through the night.

CHAPTER 8

Off to the Cave

As they walked home, they discussed their immediate plans.

'We'll be home by 11 a.m.,' said Rohan, 'then we'll all make some sandwiches for dinner tonight. Perhaps Vida and Mum will help us make some Chinese rolls, samosas, parathas and pastries. Those will last a while in our cooler.'

'Maybe we should have a nap straight after lunch,' said Anu. 'I know lunch is at noon so if we sleep from 12:30 to 3 p.m., it would help us keep awake tonight.'

'Good ideas, gang,' said Nimal. 'I'm so hungry again. It must be all this walking we're doing, and being out in the fresh air.'

'Haven't noticed you eat any less when you're indoors, yaar,' said Rohan with a chuckle, ducking quickly as Nimal took a swing at him.

When they got home they carried out their plans. Mrs. Patel had checked with Ashok and Vijay, and the two men were more than willing to help the children carry their things to the cave.

Vida and Mrs. Patel helped them make a pile of sandwiches, pastries, rolls and all kinds of other goodies, and even gave them a large chocolate cake, which Anu put in a tin so that it wouldn't get squashed. After a good lunch, they went to bed, setting their alarms to wake them at 3 p.m.

They fell asleep quickly, and woke up feeling refreshed and ready to start off on 'The Case of the Peacock Feathers', as Gina called it.

'Ashok and Vijay are downstairs with your gear,' called Mrs. Patel at 3:15. 'Come on down for a light tea.'

They trooped downstairs, all of them, including Hunter, eager to begin their adventure. This was it! They were going to spend some nights in their cave and look for crooks. Maybe they would capture those bad guys. Wouldn't everyone be pleased with them if they did?

'I made up a poem about Hunter and us,' said Gina as they sat down to tea, 'and it's not a limerick this time.'

'Well, let's hear it,' said Mrs. Patel, and the others nodded. It was unusual for the little girl to make up poetry in a form other than as a limerick.

'It's called "The Adventure Begins",' said Gina. She recited the poem she had written, pausing every now and then when they burst out laughing at her rhymes.

> Rohan, Nimal, Anu and Gina
> Were coming home from school
> When all at once they got a dog,
> And things got mighty cool.
>
> Hunter was his name, we found
> And grapes he loved to eat.
> He'd take the seeds right out of them
> With his sharp, pointed teeth.
>
> With watermelon it was fun
> To watch him eat it up.
> He'd take a piece, spit out the seeds,
> He's such a clever pup.
>
> He greeted Mum so graciously
> And picked for her a rose.
> How did he learn that funny trick?

Well, goodness only knows!

We call ourselves the 'JEACs' now
And Peter said, 'Be brave
As you go off adventuring
And sleep in your own cave.'

Our plan is quite a simple one,
We're going to catch the crooks
And all of us will sit on them,
They won't get off the hook.

We all love birds and animals
And hate to see them killed.
So watch out crooks, 'cause here we come,
The jailhouse will be filled!

As she finished, everyone stared at her in amazement. Could this be a poem made up by Gina? She certainly was getting good at fun verse. Then they applauded her loudly, and Gina grinned with pleasure. She enjoyed writing poetry, and was glad that this one was such a success.

'I'm impressed, Gina,' said her mother. 'How long did it take you to make that up?'

'About half an hour,' replied Gina. 'It's just nonsense verse.'

'It's still really good,' said Ashok. 'I hope it's written down so Jim can see it.'

'Yes, it's on a piece of paper,' said Gina. 'I'll give it to you, Mum, and you can show it to Dad.'

'You'll have to do some more,' said Anu, 'I'll give you one of my note books, and you can write more poetry while we're watching the waterhole.'

'Thanks, Anu,' said Gina. She was a bit surprised by all the support for her silly verses, but quite pleased about it, too.

'All finished?' asked Mrs. Patel looking around. As everyone nodded she continued, 'Well, children, remember not to take unnecessary risks. You know those poachers are dangerous, and I'm trusting that all of you will be sensible. Have fun, and I hope you find some clues, but do take care. Oh, and before I forget – here's another bag for your sack – just some packets of chedva and chips. I know how you kids always like something to munch.'

She gave each of them a hug, and then they loaded up – even Hunter had a small knapsack on his back, filled with bones and dog biscuits.

Off they went. They followed a narrow trail, which was invisible to the untutored eye, and unless a person was very familiar with the jungle, they would never find it. Ashok led the way and Hunter was with him so that he could sniff out any strangers, and warn them; Nimal followed, with the girls next; and Rohan and Vijay brought up the rear. It was very quiet at this time, since most of the animals were resting and would only go down to the waterholes at sunset, to refresh themselves.

The group made good progress, despite the heavy sacks, and there was no sign of anyone else moving around. As they neared the waterhole and their cave, Ashok called a halt and cautioned them to speak quietly.

'I'm just going to scout around with Hunter, to make sure there's no one near the entrance to your cave,' he murmured softly.

He left the sack with the others and set off. Hunter seemed to know instinctively what they were doing, and he walked without a sound, his nose and ears alert for any danger. They returned in ten minutes.

'All clear,' said Ashok quietly, 'but let's make it quick and soundless.'

They moved swiftly to the cave entrance; Rohan and Nimal uncovered the large hole in the tree, climbed in, and first took the sacks from Ashok and Vijay, piling them in a corner of the tunnel. Then they collected all the knapsacks and placed them with the other things, but kept their binoculars, which they hung around their necks; Anu had her camera slung around her neck.

Hunter was on guard just outside the entrance to the tunnel.

'I think it would be better if Hunter didn't come with us just now,' said Rohan, thoughtfully. 'The animals may sniff him out and get scared away; they're not yet used to dogs wandering around the HP. Also, he's sure to bark if anyone other than us entered the tunnel. What do you others think?'

They agreed with him; so Nimal called to Hunter from inside the tunnel. The dog jumped in and looked up at the boys.

'On guard, Hunter,' said Rohan, pointing to their gear.

Hunter looked at the pile and immediately sat down in front of it. He wagged his tail as if to say, 'Don't worry. No one will be able to take anything while I'm here.'

The boys climbed out, after patting Hunter and praising him. They gave him some biscuits and he watched them wistfully as they left, but did not budge from his post.

Quickly covering up the entrance once more, the JEACs moved away silently, till they were at the opposite end of the waterhole. Ashok and Vijay wished them good luck, and made their way back home. Chattering loudly to one another, the children went down to the waterhole.

'Here's a good spot from where we can watch the animals,' said Rohan to the others. 'We'll sit on this log, behind the trees.'

'Good idea,' agreed Anu, as she and the others moved to join him.

'Use your binoculars to look around,' whispered Rohan, once they were all seated on the log, 'but make comments as if you're looking for animals.'

'Aye, aye, Captain,' mumbled Nimal softly. He put his binoculars to his eyes and looked up towards their cave. He would not have been able to guess it existed if he didn't know about it; it was so well hidden. He looked towards the big tree which hid the entrance to their cave, and scanned the area closely. 'No signs of any animals coming down yet,' he said loudly, 'I wonder what time they'll be here?'

'Oh, not till sunset,' said Rohan, looking carefully at another area near the waterhole. 'We still have half an hour to wait, but keep your eyes peeled – you never know what birds or animals may come early.' He didn't see anything suspicious either.

Anu was looking back into the jungle. She suddenly saw something red in a bush slightly to her right, about fifteen metres behind them. Although her heart raced, she kept her cool; casually turning her binoculars away as if she hadn't noticed anything she said loudly, 'I don't see a thing either, but please change places with me, Rohan; I'm tired of looking behind – it's so boring.'

Rohan looked at her in surprise, but changed places. As she brushed past him she whispered, under pretext of wiping her face with her handkerchief, 'In the large green bush to the right, next to the big tamarind tree – something red – check it out! I think we're being watched.'

Rohan sat down casually and looked up into the treetops for a few moments. 'I think some of the monkeys are waking up,' he said loudly to the others. 'We should see some action shortly.'

Then, looking through his binoculars, he turned his head very slowly, carefully examining the bush Anu had told him about, without lingering on it for too long. 'Nothing else,' he said to the others. 'Maybe we'd better talk softly though, in case we scare away any animals on their way here.'

He turned back and whispered to the others. 'Don't turn around – Anu noticed us being observed – here's the plan. Lie down on your stomachs behind this log, as if we're engrossed in watching the waterhole. Excellent! There are a few deer coming down now.'

The others obeyed him quickly, and he continued softly. 'There are two men in the bush – one in a brown shirt with a red scarf, and the other in a dull yellow, shirt – I can't see their faces, but they must be the crooks. They don't seem to have any binoculars with them at the moment. Once a few animals come down, and we've watched them for a bit, I'll get up and say it's time to go home. We'll move away from the waterhole – and then just follow my lead. Got it?'

'Yeah,' muttered Nimal excitedly. 'I'm sure those chaps won't move.'

They watched the waterhole in silence, and after a while, a few more small animals, monkeys and birds came down to the water. Once they had drunk their fill and dispersed, and before any other creatures came down, Rohan stood up.

'Okay, gang,' he said loudly, looking at his watch, 'we'd better head for home before Mum sends out the search party – let's wrap it up.'

'But can't we stay a bit longer?' cried Gina, pretending she was very keen on hanging around.

'Gina, your mum did tell us not to stay out too long,' said Nimal. 'We can always come back another day. I'm just going to check if there are any more creatures coming down to drink.' He put his binoculars to his eyes once more and scanned the entire area of the jungle around them. 'Nothing to be seen,' he said, and as he bent to give Gina a hand up he whispered to the others, 'They're still there.'

'Let's follow the old trail,' said Anu. 'You know, the one opposite us – it leads right back home.'

'Good idea, let's move, JEACs,' said Rohan.

They set off, chatting to each other, and using the animals as an excuse to keep looking through their binoculars every now and then.

'We're not being followed,' said Rohan softly, as they reached the big tree leading to their cave. 'The men are still in that bush so we'll carry on up the trail for a bit. They won't be able to see us, but they may be able to hear our voices, and if they see the bushes shaking on the trail, they'll think we've gone.'

So they went up the trail, deliberately talking loudly and shaking the bushes, and then stopped and hid in the undergrowth close to the entrance of their cave.

'I'll slip back to the tree,' said Rohan softly, 'and if they're still in the bush, I'll give the "owl" signal, and you can get into the tunnel as fast as possible. I'll join you shortly. Don't let Hunter make a sound.'

The others nodded, and Rohan crept back to the tree quietly. Finding a safe spot, he used his binoculars to look at the bush, which was right opposite him. He saw the two men, still in hiding, but they were no longer watching the trail – they were looking at the creatures coming to the waterhole. They obviously thought that the children had gone and were not at all threatened by the fact that they had been so close to them.

Rohan hooted like an owl and quickly went back to the tree. He found that Nimal and the girls had gone in, just ahead of him, and Nimal was whispering to Hunter to be quiet.

Rohan entered the tunnel and said softly, 'The men are still there, but who knows how long they'll stay in the bush. Anu, you and Gina go straight to the cave, quietly, and watch to see what the men do; Nimal, help me cover this entrance carefully, so that they can't find us. Hurry!'

The girls ran down the tunnel; the hole in the tree led to a wide passageway, which ran underground for about four metres, before turning into a large cave – divided in two. The first room was at the back of the cave, and large enough to put down four sleeping bags and store the food and lanterns; the second space was smaller, and opened out above the waterhole – three and a half metres below. The opening, which was wide enough for four or five people to peer out at the same time, was completely covered by thick branches from a large tree to its left, and a heavy fringe of creepers. It was totally invisible from outside, unless you knew exactly where to look, but a little light filtered in from small gaps in the covering. Nobody could possibly climb up to the cave since, firstly, the waterhole was right beneath it and, secondly, the slope from the waterhole to the cave was extremely steep. A clear, shallow stream flowed into the waterhole. The cave was definitely a great hideout.

Anu lit a lantern at the back of the cave, which shed enough light for them to see what they were doing, but did not filter out of their hiding place.

The girls lay down and peered out, using their binoculars. They did not need to part the covering at all since the gaps were sufficient for them to look through.

'There they are, Gina,' muttered Anu under her breath. 'To your right – in that green and yellow bush.'

'Okay, I've got them,' whispered Gina.

'Too bad I haven't loaded high-speed film into my camera yet; I could have taken a couple of pictures, but at the moment I'd have to use a flash and those guys would see it,' said Anu.

'Oh, they're leaving,' exclaimed Gina. 'I do hope the boys have finished covering the entrance.'

'I think I hear the boys and Hunter,' said Anu. 'Here they are. Hurry, you two, the men are leaving,' she called softly.

The boys flung themselves down and watched as the men emerged from the bush and walk away from the waterhole. Unfortunately, the JEACs could not see the crooks' faces, but noticed that the man with the red scarf was of medium height and very skinny, while the man in the yellow shirt was short, broad and tough-looking. They both wore dirty denim jeans and carried guns.

CHAPTER 9

Settling, Spying, Sleeping

As soon as the crooks were out of sight, the children sat up and looked at each other in excitement.

'Should we try and follow them now?' asked Nimal impulsively.

'No, I don't think so,' said Rohan thoughtfully. 'We'll be better off doing that tomorrow or at night – it's still not dark enough and they may wonder if we're still close by.'

'Okay, then let's get everything in from the passage and set up the cave,' said Anu, who was eager to settle in. 'Did you bring an alarm clock, Rohan?'

'No, I thought we could use the one on my watch – it'll be less noisy than a regular alarm clock. Nimal also has an alarm on his watch. Okay, JEACs, let's get moving. I think, however, that we should leave someone here to keep an eye open, just in case those chaps come back.'

'Also, someone should listen for them near the entrance,' said Anu. 'We don't want them to hear us walking up and down and talking in the passageway, even though I know the tunnel and the cave are pretty soundproof.'

'Good idea, Anu,' said Nimal. 'Hunter can guard the entrance till we've moved everything, and maybe Gina could watch the waterhole. What do you say, Gina?'

'I don't mind,' said Gina immediately. She loved being given responsibilities like that.

'Let's take Hunter and put him on guard,' said Rohan, 'and just to be on the safe side, maybe we should talk in whispers as we move up and down and not make a noise. Anu, why don't you stay here; Nimal and I will bring up the sacks and you can arrange the things.'

'Okey-dokey, no problemo,' said Anu, who loved to arrange things neatly – it was *keeping* them neat for a long period of time that she found tough.

The boys went off with Hunter and put the dog on guard while they carried their things to the cave.

'Good thing this cave is like two rooms,' said Anu to Gina, as she unrolled sleeping bags and placed them on one side of the first section.

'Yes, and it's also nice to have those ledges on the wall; they make great shelves for all our food and pots and pans.'

'That's the lot,' said Rohan as he and Nimal returned with Hunter and the final load. 'Not a sound from outside.'

Anu had arranged most of their things by then.

'Here are the special clothes,' said Nimal unpacking the last sack. 'And, *voilà*! The umbrella!' He fished out the umbrella which was right at the bottom. 'Goodo!'

'Oooh, what a strange-looking umbrella,' said Anu, spotting the parrot's head and reaching out for it.

Nimal handed it over and he and Rohan watched as Anu looked it over, wondering if she would notice the tape covering the second button; but she was more interested in the parrot's head handle, and did not see anything else unusual.

'I just can't *believe* you're carrying an umbrella all over the place, Rohan,' said Anu. 'Oh, well – guess we all have some strange quirks. Here you are.' She handed it back.

'Well, it's so unusual,' said Rohan, placing the umbrella on top of his sleeping bag. 'Now, where do you want this water cooler placed?' he asked, smoothly changing the topic of conversation.

'Just over here, thanks,' said Anu, pointing to a spot near the shelves. 'This is our kitchen, dining and sleeping area, and our little stove is all set up, too.'

'I must say our cave looks nice and cosy,' said Rohan, looking around. 'We have a bedroom, a kitchen, a library and a balcony with a view. Who could ask for more?'

The others laughed and agreed it was a superb place to have.

Hunter, who had sniffed curiously around the entire cave, now gave a huge sigh and settled down near them.

'I think he approves of our cave,' said Nimal with a laugh, patting the dog.

'Gina, I think we're fine now,' said Rohan. 'Even if those guys come back, they'll never guess we're here – just as long as we talk normally and don't shout.'

'Yeah, it's kind of neat, isn't it?' said Nimal. 'I couldn't believe it when we tested it last time and discovered that while inside the cave, we could hear the slightest noise from the waterhole or surrounding area, but when we were out there, we couldn't hear voices coming from inside the cave – unless they were exceptionally loud.'

'Well, luckily for us it works that way,' said Rohan. 'I think, though, that when it gets darker outside and we have to light the lanterns or the cooker, we should put a sheet over the opening so that no light can filter through. Why take unnecessary risks?'

'Good idea, yaar,' said Nimal. 'Now, how about dinner, Anu, I'm ...' He stopped with a laugh as the others chorused 'starved!' 'Okay! Okay!' he chuckled, 'I know I always say that, but at least I'm honest about it. Aren't you hungry, too?'

The others admitted they were, so they got out the food and started on a delicious meal.

'Why is it that food always tastes *extra* good and you can eat tons of it when you're doing something secret, like a midnight feast, or hiding away, or on a picnic?' asked Nimal, munching away hungrily. 'I could eat like an elephant.'

'You always say that, too, Nimal,' said Gina with a grin. 'But I've never noticed you eat any less at other times.'

She ducked as Nimal threw his napkin at her. Hunter enjoyed his meal. He was a bit puzzled as to why they were in this strange place, all hidden away, but as long as he was with them, he was perfectly happy.

'Now for the chocolate cake,' said Gina, as they finished off their meal with bottles of lemonade. 'I'll get it,' she offered, getting up and going to the shelf on which Anu had arranged everything neatly. She handed the tin to Anu.

'Nimal, I'm sure you're too full to eat any cake,' teased Anu. 'I'll save your piece for tomorrow, shall I?'

'No way – don't you dare,' growled Nimal in tones of deep injury. 'Knowing Gina's capacity for chocolate cake, I'm sure there'll be a feast while I'm asleep, and the cake would have vanished by morning.'

They chuckled at his indignation, and Anu gave everyone a large slice of cake. Then they put away the food, piling the dishes neatly in the tunnel, ready to be washed in the stream later on, when it was darker.

'It's quite early yet,' said Rohan lounging back lazily, 'what do you feel like doing?' He looked around at everyone.

'Well, I'd love to watch some of the animals for a bit,' said Gina.

'And I want to read one of the new books and make some notes,' said Anu, picking up the book called *Planet Zoo*, and grinning at the others half apologetically.

'We understand, Anu – you need some space, right?' said Nimal with a laugh that the others joined in. 'I need a nap,' he added. 'After all, I'll be up for part of the night; what about you, Rohan? You should get some more sleep, too, you know.'

'I guess so,' said Rohan, 'but I do want to read my new book on detectives for a while. 'Gina, we'll cover up most of the opening, leaving a gap through which you can see the waterhole. Then we can light one bright lantern at the back of the cave so that Anu and I can read. Nimal, set your alarm for 10 p.m. and I'll do the same.'

'Boy, are you ever organized, Rohan,' said Anu.

'Well, if I want to be a good detective, I have to be thorough and organized – so I'm trying,' said Rohan with a grin.

They got everything ready and settled down. After a while, Rohan went to sleep, too, and Gina put away her binoculars and snuggled into her sleeping bag after watching for half an hour. Anu made some notes on story ideas, then turned off the lantern and went to sleep. Hunter knew he had to sleep with one eye and one ear alert, in case of danger, so he lay down near the opening.

Peace reigned in the little cave. The only noises Hunter heard were those of the animals coming to the waterhole for a drink, and he knew they were no threat to his family. The children slept till the alarms on their watches woke Rohan and Nimal, and they roused the girls.

'Anu, could you light a lantern, please? It's pitch dark,' said Rohan, 'and you know exactly where they are.'

'Actually, I placed one by my sleeping bag,' said Anu, quickly lighting a lantern. 'I figured we'd need it as soon as we woke up.'

'Good thinking, sis,' said Rohan.

CHAPTER 10

A Nasty Shock!

They all stood up and stretched, gratefully accepting the water that Anu handed around.

Rohan thought for a moment and then said, 'Okay, here's what we'll do for tonight. Nimal and I will scout around the two waterholes closest to this one; we'll take the walkie-talkies and our torches but won't use the torches unless it's absolutely essential, since we don't want to be seen. We'll search for a couple of hours and then come back. That means, by the time we go to the waterholes and return, it'll be around 1:30 a.m. In the meantime, you girls watch this waterhole.'

'And, of course, Hunter will be here with the girls,' said Nimal.

'Everyone okay with the plan?' said Rohan. They nodded in agreement. Rohan looked at Gina, who was dozing off; she found it hard to keep up with the older ones at times, but didn't like being left out of their activities.

'You know, Gina,' he said, 'maybe you should go to sleep again.' He continued hurriedly as the little girl sat up and gave him an indignant look. 'If you sleep now, and Anu keeps watch over the waterhole, then when we come back and need to sleep, you can keep watch for us.'

'Oh, all right,' said Gina, satisfied with the explanation and pleased with the plan of action. 'That's a good idea.'

She snuggled down into her sleeping bag again. The boys quickly put on their green and brown clothing so that there would be no likelihood of being seen if the men happened to be around.

'Bring the umbrella, Rohan,' said Nimal, winking at him. 'You never know, it might rain and at least you won't get wet.'

The girls stared at him in surprise.

'But Nimal, I've never known Rohan to be scared of a little rain before,' said Anu. 'Most of the time you boys want to go out and run around when it *is* raining and then you come back soaking wet.'

'Oh, well,' said Nimal in a lofty tone of voice, while Rohan just listened with a grin, 'I guess he's growing up and doesn't want his hair to get wet.'

The others chuckled.

'Put a sock in it, yaar,' said Rohan, 'you know they'll never buy that. Actually,' he said, turning to the girls and trying to nullify their curiosity about the umbrella, 'it'll be something we can use in defence. If we're attacked we could at least poke someone in the ribs with it and wind them a bit so that we can run away.' He picked up the umbrella.

'Now that sounds more like it,' said Gina yawning. 'Nimal, why do you always try to con us?'

'Because you rise to the bait so easily, mon enfant,' said Nimal with a grin.

'Are you ready?' asked Rohan. 'Anu, don't do anything dangerous. If you see the men and want to take pictures, get the best shots you can from here.'

'Okay, chief,' said Anu. 'Good luck, you two. See you in a couple of hours.'

'G'night and be careful,' said Gina sleepily. 'See you later.'

'Hunter, stay,' said Nimal, as the dog jumped up to go with them.

Hunter immediately went and stood by Anu and licked her hand, understanding that the boys were going out and they wanted him to protect the girls. He whined softly and wagged his tail. The boys patted him, and then, waving goodbye to the girls, went down the tunnel to the exit, each carrying a walkie-talkie. They paused for a few moments, listening for any sound outside, and then crept out quietly and carefully covered the entrance before they set out.

Gina fell asleep again.

Anu pulled her sleeping bag to the front of the cave so that she could lie in it and look out over the waterhole. She had her binoculars and camera right beside her, the camera now loaded with fast film so she would not have to use a flash in the dark. It was a beautiful, clear night, and the three-quarter moon was shining brightly, right above the waterhole. Some of the nocturnal animals were coming down to drink and Anu could see them clearly. Every now and then she scanned the jungle around the waterhole, watching for any movement not caused by animals. Sometimes she would look through her binoculars, both at the jungle and at the animals. However, nothing unusual happened.

Then she heard the raucous cry of a peacock from high above in a tree. 'Helllp! Helllp!' it cried. A few more birds called out and she saw some of them fly down.

'Oh, dear, here come the peacocks,' she muttered to herself, as the birds went down to the waterhole.

Anu kept her eyes on the jungle, hoping that no one would try to kill the beautiful birds. 'There's nothing I can do if the men do come to this waterhole tonight,' she said softly to Hunter who was lying beside her. Her voice was anxious and he licked her hand sympathetically, sensing that she was worried about something. The peacocks were very cautious and nervous of all sounds.

All of a sudden, a gunshot rang out, and then another. They sounded as if they were nearby, but none of the peacocks she was watching were harmed. However, all the creatures at the waterhole rushed back into the forest, the peacocks immediately flying up into the trees. Anu's heart raced. What had happened? Were the shots near the boys? Were they safe? She waited anxiously, listening for their return.

***

When the boys left the cave earlier, they were looking forward to their night adventures.

'Nimal, let's walk along this trail together until we come to the fork where it divides,' suggested Rohan, 'and then you go to one waterhole and I'll cover the other.'

'Okay,' said Nimal, 'but don't you think it would be better if we walked in the undergrowth beside the trail – just in case there are others using the trail, too?'

'Super idea,' said Rohan, 'we'll have to walk really softly, and not make a sound, otherwise the purpose will be lost.'

'Of course,' agreed Nimal who, while in general was a real klutz, could be dead silent when tracking animals to observe them, or when he was trying to persuade an animal to come to him.

Having grown up on the Conservation and observing creatures from the time they were very young, Nimal, Rohan and the girls had all practised walking extremely quietly in the jungle, and it had served them well in the past. The boys merged into the jungle easily.

It was a typical night in the jungle with the sounds of animals calling to one another, while a slight breeze made the trees whisper in a shushing tone. A tiger, in the CH area, roared in anger at losing his prey, while an elephant trumpeted loudly to its herd.

'Rohan,' whispered Nimal suddenly, 'where are you?'

'I'm right here in front of you, dummy,' murmured Rohan softly, turning around. He was about a metre ahead of Nimal.

'Boy, you sure gave me a scare,' gasped Nimal in relief. 'You know, these clothes really are something. Till you turned around and I saw your face, I couldn't see you at all – you totally merge with the surroundings.'

'Good,' said Rohan, 'so do you. We'll certainly need the camouflage if we meet those crooks. By the way, when we've checked out our waterholes, maybe we'd better use the walkie-talkies to make sure we're both okay and are heading back to the cave – and use the ear phones, yaar.'

'Yeah, otherwise we may be spooked by each other,' said Nimal with a soft chuckle.

They continued on their way, surprising a few animals that promptly moved out of their way. At the fork of the trail, the boys stopped for a moment.

'All right on your own?' asked Rohan. 'At the first sign of trouble, use the walkie-talkie.'

'Sure, no problemo,' whispered Nimal. 'See you back at the cave entrance by 1:15 a.m.'

They synchronized their watches, put in their earpieces so that *only they* could hear them beep, and then parted.

Nimal went left and soon found the waterhole he was to keep an eye on. He scouted the area quickly, in case there was a prowler already hanging around it, pausing to pet some rabbits and a hedgehog that came up to him. Finding a comfortable bush close to the waterhole, he squashed himself into it. He knew he would be quite safe and not easily spotted since the animals came near him and sat close by without being scared off. With a rabbit cuddled on his lap, he scanned the area with his binoculars, but there was nothing to be seen or heard other than the usual jungle sounds.

Rohan turned right at the fork and went to the other waterhole, which was a very small one, making sure that he did not alert anyone who might be watching, and treading carefully to avoid dry twigs. He saw a few creatures at the waterhole, drinking water and nosing around for food. There was very little moonlight shining over the waterhole, since the canopy of trees covered it more or less completely, and as the moon was not directly over the area, only a faint glow lit it up. Making his way around and keeping to the undergrowth, he found a thick stumpy tree with heavy, dark green, branches which drooped right to the ground.

'The perfect spot for hiding,' thought Rohan as he crept under it and settled down quietly. He had an excellent view of the waterhole.

Sometime later, he yawned and looked at his watch. It was half past midnight and nothing had moved, other than the few deer, wild boar and jackals, which had come to the waterhole for a drink. He was just about to creep out and go in search of Nimal, when he noticed some peacocks come down to the water. They had barely started drinking when a gunshot rang out and one of the peacocks dropped dead. Another gunshot sounded immediately after the first one, but the other peacocks had flown up into the trees immediately, and only the one bird was killed.

Rohan sat motionless with shock. He had not seen any movement of men approaching the waterhole, and he knew he would have noticed anything immediately. As he watched in horrified silence, he saw a man with a red scarf come out of the undergrowth a few metres to his left, run down to the waterhole, pick up the peacock and disappear into the jungle. The man had a gun.

Rohan's walkie-talkie beeped softly in his ear, and he pushed the button in a daze.

'Rohan, are you okay?' came Nimal's voice in an agitated whisper. 'I heard gunshots. Were they near you? What's happening? Over.'

'I'm fine,' said Rohan a little shakily, holding the walkie-talkie close to his mouth and speaking in a whisper. 'Those brutes killed another peacock at this waterhole. There was only one man. Look, stay where you are for five minutes, and then come over here. Be extremely careful, don't get on the trail or make any noise at all since this chap may still be in the vicinity. I'm under a strange-looking tree which has dark green branches drooping down to the ground on the north side of the waterhole. Over.'

'Right,' said Nimal, 'I'll be there in fifteen minutes. Over and out.'

The walkie-talkies went off the air, and Rohan crouched in his shelter, feeling very angry and helpless – it had all happened so fast. Nimal arrived so quietly that Rohan jumped when he felt someone creeping in beside him.

'Only me, yaar,' said Nimal, 'Man, that must have been horrible.'

'It was,' said Rohan, and gave Nimal the details. 'Did you hear or see anything as you were coming?' The boy's voice was shaking with anger.

'Nothing at all,' said Nimal. 'Those chaps must be pretty good at tracking. Okay, what should we do now?'

'Well, the man came out of the bushes to my left,' said Rohan, 'so I think we should make our way over there and check to see if there are any clues to be found.'

They moved round the waterhole cautiously, and arrived at the spot from which Rohan had seen the man emerge. They checked the ground carefully for anything that might be a clue, but it was practically impossible to see in the faint moonlight, especially as they did not want to use their torches, so they had to give up.

'We'll just have to come back in the day time,' said Rohan in exasperation.

'Shall we make our way back to the cave, then?' queried Nimal. 'Anu would have heard the shots, too, and she'll be worried – wondering if we're safe.'

'Sure,' said Rohan, 'we can't do anything at the moment. It just makes me so angry that I couldn't do a thing to stop that bird from being killed. We've simply got to catch those crooks.'

'We will, don't you worry,' said Nimal consolingly. He knew he would have felt equally bad if he had been in Rohan's shoes.

Rohan had a temper, which he rarely lost, but Nimal could tell that he was having a hard time controlling it at the moment. However, by the time they reached the cave, Rohan had regained his cool; there were no further incidents and the boys entered the cave quietly.

Anu and Hunter heard them coming back and greeted them with relief.

'I was really scared,' said Anu, as she quickly prepared hot drinks, which the boys gulped down gratefully.

They told her what had happened and then tumbled into their sleeping bags – it was 1:30 in the morning.

'I don't think it's worth waking Gina at this time – I doubt the men will come to this waterhole tonight,' said Rohan. 'But we should try and get up by 5 a.m. and check that area thoroughly.'

'Okay – well, goodnight, you two,' said Anu, 'It's been a horrid night but I'm glad at least you're both safe.'

'I'll set my alarm and wake all of you,' said Nimal as he cuddled into his sleeping bag with Hunter lying on his feet.

CHAPTER 11

Clues!

The JEACs slept soundly and were up at 5 a.m. After a quick drink of juice – during which time they told Gina of the happenings at night and why they didn't wake her – they were ready to set off.

'It's 5:30,' said Rohan, looking at his watch, 'and it's a good time to search for clues. I must say we all look pretty much like part of the forest in our jungle clothes, and it'll be tough for anyone to spot us.'

'What should we take other than my camera and Nimal's sketch pad?' asked Anu.

'Well, we have the umbrella, too,' said Nimal, 'and our binocs.'

'And I have a bag in which to put clues,' said Gina. She was disappointed that the others had had an adventure without her, and was determined to find lots of clues to make up. 'If we catch the crooks, I'll put them in the bag, too,' she added fiercely.

The others laughed as they made their way to the entrance and out of the hole in the tree, covering it up behind them as usual. This time Hunter came with them.

They marked some signs on the tree, as promised, so that Mr. Patel would know they were safe.

'Be careful, and tread softly,' said Rohan, leading the way. 'I'm not going to walk on the trail, so watch out for twigs and branches.'

Reaching the waterhole shortly, they hid under the tree Rohan had found the previous night.

'Rohan,' whispered Nimal, 'why don't Hunter and I scout round the waterhole – as if we were just out for a stroll – and see if the men are hiding around here, hoping to get some more birds? I'm sure Hunter will sniff them out fast enough.'

'Good idea,' said Rohan.

Nimal and Hunter stepped out and walked around the area, but Hunter, though he sniffed at all the bushes, did not growl once. Nimal signalled to the others that it was safe and they emerged from hiding.

'Let's split up,' suggested Nimal, 'so that we can search a wider area in less time. I'll go down to the water and see if there are any footprints and make sketches of them.'

'Okay,' said Rohan. 'Anu, you and I will search on either side of this large tree and Gina, you search those bushes. I know the man came out from somewhere around here.'

'We'd better work quietly,' Anu reminded the others. 'You never know if those chaps will come back and hear us. Don't yell if you find a clue. Just hoot like an owl and we'll join you.'

'Hunter will also warn us if anyone approaches,' said Nimal.

'Good – and if Hunter growls or barks, just pretend that you're interested in animal footprints, or something, and call out accordingly,' said Rohan.

They set to work while Hunter nosed around the edge of the waterhole, and then sat down to watch them.

Nimal was the first to find a clue. He hooted softly, and the others made their way down to where he was squatting near the water with his sketch pad out and his pencil working swiftly.

'Look at these two footprints,' he exclaimed in excitement. 'They're so clear and easy to copy.'

'Great work, Nimal,' said Rohan, 'wish I could draw like that. Now we just need to match the prints with the shoes, when we find any, and that'll help in a court case to prove who the culprits are.'

'I'm going to take a couple of pictures, as well,' said Anu, pulling out her camera and clicking busily.

They left Nimal to finish his sketch, and went back to their search.

Gina was looking among the bushes when she suddenly saw something red stuck on a thorny bush. She pulled it off and studied it for a moment. Then, in great excitement, she hooted like an owl. The others immediately joined her.

Eyes glowing eagerly, she said, 'Look what I found in the bushes. It's a piece of red cloth – I think it must be from that man's scarf. Didn't you say his scarf was red, Rohan?'

'It sure was,' said Rohan. 'Excellent work, Gina – this is a smashing clue. Put it in your bag.'

The little girl was thrilled and put the piece of cloth into her bag.

The others also began to look around the area where the cloth was found, in case they discovered any other clues that the man may have left behind.

'Oooh, look,' said Anu, picking up something carefully with a leaf, 'two cigarette butts. Gina, open the bag, please.'

'And this round impression again,' said Rohan. 'Nimal, where's your sketch pad? You have more work; Anu, take a couple of pictures, too, I'm sure it was from a bag.'

Nimal finished his sketching and then noticed a small spot, which looked as if the earth had been dug up and then covered over again recently. Using a stick he carefully uncovered the area.

'Well, well, well! See what I've found,' he said, showing them an empty can of ham. 'I guess our crook must have been hiding here for quite a while before you came down, Rohan. Good thing he didn't see you – you must have been dead quiet.'

He added the can to Gina's collecting bag.

They continued searching for about half an hour more, but did not find anything else, so they agreed to return to their cave and discuss the matter further. Reaching the cave without any problem, they prepared breakfast and then sat down to discuss the situation while eating.

'You know, these clues will be used in the court case to prove that the men were actually the crooks,' said Rohan, thoughtfully. 'Naturally, one of the best clues would be if we could get a picture of them in action, but that may be rather hard to do.'

'Yes, and so far Haren, Bill and you, have all seen these guys, but they always disappear and none of us know where their hideout is,' grumbled Nimal.

'Can't we go and look for it?' asked Gina eagerly.

'We don't even know where to start at the moment,' said Anu slowly, 'but I've been thinking.' She hesitated.

'Cough it up, Anu,' said Rohan. He knew she had an orderly mind where coming up with plans was concerned.

'Okay,' said Anu. 'These chaps seem to know exactly where Dad's men are stationed, and then they go to the other waterholes. Now, obviously, they don't know we're camping out in the jungle near this large waterhole. Also, they may have decided not to come here last night because they saw us playing around here and thought the peacocks may not come down to our waterhole – you know – in case we had scared the birds away. When they remember that no one came running to catch them when they fired their gun last night, I think they'll feel safer about this whole area, and they may come back to this waterhole either tonight or tomorrow night – after all, it's the largest in the area and the peacocks do come here often. So here's my proposal.'

She paused, looked at the others, and continued when Rohan said encouragingly, 'Go on, Anu. Your thoughts are very clear and logical, as usual.'

The others nodded in agreement.

'Thanks! I think we should watch this waterhole all night for the next couple of nights. If we see the crooks let's try and take some pictures, and also follow them. My idea is that Gina and I watch from the cave, taking turns to sleep, and you two boys stay together in the bushes near the waterhole. Leave one walkie-talkie with us and take the other with you, and then, if we see something, we'll alert you and decide what to do next. And, boys, if they *do* kill a bird, try not to get too mad or do something stupid – especially you, Rohan – I know what you're like when you lose your temper. Remember, they have guns – I really believe you should both stick together for the time being.'

'Okay, okay, Grandma,' said Nimal with a grin. 'We solemnly promise not to be stupid. But do continue – this gets more and more interesting, and you have a great plan so far.'

'Right. As soon as the crooks start moving away from the waterhole, we'll warn you over the walkie-talkie; and you can trail them cautiously. I'm sure they'll go straight to their hideout – since they'll wonder if any of the staff heard the gun – and if you discover where it is, come back here and we'll all go and fetch Dad and Mike to catch them.'

'It sounds like a fantastic plan, Anu, and I'm positive it'll work well,' said Rohan after he had mulled it over. 'Let's go for it.'

'Should we perhaps leave a message for Peter to tell him what we've found so far?' asked Nimal. 'I could run over to his place and tell Mrs. Collins to pass on the information to Peter, Dad and Mike.'

'Yeah, that's a good idea,' said Rohan, looking at his watch. 'It's now 8 o'clock, and you should try and get back by 10:30 at the latest. Then we can get some sleep before we follow through with our plans. Also, I don't think we should play around too much, in the open, in case the crooks see us and get suspicious – so let's do something in here.'

'Good,' said Anu, 'I like that. I want to catch up on some of my writing and reading. I hardly have time to read in school, other than text books of course.'

'And I'm going to write a poem and play my flute softly,' said Gina.

'Well, I'm going to change first,' said Rohan 'and then make notes of what we've discovered so far.'

'I'm off, then,' said Nimal. 'I think I'll take Hunter with me; stick to the main trail and make a big noise as I go, whistling and singing – that way, if the crooks see me, they won't worry about a noisy boy and his dog.'

'Oh, no,' said Anu in mock dismay. 'You'll scare off all the birds and animals for miles around.' She dodged as Nimal threw a pillow at her.

Nimal and Hunter set off, and the others, once they had covered the opening of the cave with a curtain to make sure no light got out even in the day time, settled down to their various activities.

'Do we need to keep watch just now, Rohan?' asked Anu.

'No, I'm sure those chaps are sleeping and will keep a low profile during the day time because they know the staff will be wandering around,' said Rohan. 'We should start keeping watch around 4 p.m.'

'Goodo,' said Anu, curling up on her sleeping bag with a notebook. 'I must admit it's nice to have two lanterns in the cave. We have more than enough light for working in.'

'Gina, you've improved a great deal since I last heard you,' said Rohan to the little girl, who was playing her flute softly.

'I've been practising like crazy,' said Gina, pausing for a moment. 'A snake charmer has to be very good, because snakes like music a lot, and if you play the wrong notes, they'll bite you.'

Rohan and Anu laughed.

'Where did you hear that from, Gina?' asked Anu curiously.

'My music teacher told me,' said Gina in all seriousness, and she went back to playing.

Rohan winked at Anu and she grinned back. Neither said anything to disillusion the little girl – she would discover the truth for herself soon enough as she read many books about animals. They all settled down and peace reigned in the cave, with background music by Gina.

After a while, Gina stopped playing the flute, curled up with her new notebook and a pencil, and started writing.

'There's Nimal,' said Rohan sometime later. 'I can hear his footsteps in the tunnel.'

'Hi, all,' said Nimal coming into the cave with Hunter. 'No incidents either going or coming – we didn't hear or see anyone on the trail at all. I left a message for Peter and the APs and made it back really fast; it's only 10 a.m.'

Hunter was busy greeting the others as if he had not seen them for years.

'Great!' said Rohan. 'Did anyone have any news for us?'

'Nope,' said Nimal. 'But I do have a delish parcel of food from Aunty Nancy, who doesn't want us to starve in our cave – another chocolate cake, and a whole batch of large, Punjabi samosas.'

He passed the food to Anu who put it away after handing out a samosa to each of them.

'And now, ladies and germ, I'm going to have a nap,' continued Nimal. He curled up in his sleeping bag and yawned loudly. 'Wake me up for lunch, somebody.'

His yawns set Anu and Rohan off, and after setting his alarm, Rohan soon fell asleep, too, Anu following suit shortly thereafter. Gina turned off one lantern; she wasn't tired since she had had a good night's sleep; so she finished off her poem, which was about the clues they had found, and then read for a while.

At around 1 p.m., she became hungry and thought the others would wake up soon and want some lunch, so she rose softly and set about making a pile of sandwiches, took out the fresh samosas sent by Mrs. Collins and put on some eggs to boil. The smell of the food and the friendly sound of bubbling water in the pan woke Nimal. He stretched and rose to help Gina.

'Mmmm. I'm starved, Gina,' whispered Nimal as he cut up the sandwiches she was making. 'How nice of you to get lunch ready for us, kiddo.'

'Well, I hope the sandwiches are okay,' said Gina a trifle anxiously.

'Why don't I taste one for you?' said Nimal promptly, picking up a ham sandwich and eating it quickly. 'Oh, boy! That was simply delish! Can I have another – pleeease?'

Gina giggled and gave him another sandwich just as Rohan and Anu woke up.

They were all hungry and quickly finished the food that Gina had prepared; ending their meal with a slice of chocolate cake each. Naturally, Hunter got his share. They loved to spoil him and, though he was never greedy, he enjoyed the food very much indeed.

'Do you want to hear my new poem?' asked Gina after they had cleared away the things and were planning to settle down to a game of cards.

'You mean you've finished yet another one?' asked Rohan in amazement. 'Boy – do you ever work fast!'

'It's just a short one,' said Gina modestly, 'and it's about the clues and things we've done so far.'

'Well, let's hear it, genius,' said Nimal.

'Yes,' said Anu encouragingly. 'Go ahead, sis.'

'Okay! Here goes,' said Gina. 'It's called "On the Hunt".'

You've heard before, I'm very sure,
Of us JEACs – we total five!
We have set out, without a doubt
To catch those crooks alive.

The very first night, we got a fright,
When gunshots we did hear.

Then Rohan saw a man for sure,
Who killed a peacock near.

Oh, we were mad, and very sad
To hear this awful news.
So off we got, to the fatal spot
And searched like mad for clues.

Nimal and Anu had more fun, too,
Drawing and taking snaps
Of footprints made, and round bag laid
By that nasty man who zaps.

Then Gina found, quite near the ground,
A piece of scarf, quite red.
Near Nimal's feet was a can of meat,
Off which the crook had fed.

Determined we are not to let this go far,
Those crooks we sure will catch.
They'd better beware, and have a care
For us they are no match!

They all applauded when she finished reciting her latest composition.

'Boy, I sure wish I could spout off verse like you do, Gina,' said Nimal enviously. 'I would make up verses about Mohan and the other crazy things that happen in school.'

'You get better and better each time,' said Anu. 'I can see that you're improving your rhythm and are using all kinds of different verse forms now. Good for you. I think you should keep on doing this, kiddo!'

'One of the things I like best is the way in which you manage to put all the main points of what has happened into the poem, and it's still hilarious,' said Rohan, giving her a hug.

'When we plan our mission statement, and goals and objectives for the JEACs, we should give you all the facts, Gina, and you can put them into verse form,' said Anu. 'I doubt many other organizations have anything like that. Or, better still, let's have a theme song.'

'Excellent ideas,' agreed Rohan and Nimal; and Gina glowed with pleasure.

'Well, here's to the budding poetess,' said Nimal, pouring out mugs of lemonade, and they all raised their mugs to Gina who was thrilled to bits.

CHAPTER 12

An All Night Wake

They settled down to pass away the rest of the afternoon playing cards and board games, reading, writing and chatting.

'I've found a new word,' said Anu, looking up from the book she was reading. 'It's in *Planet Zoo* – "biophilia".'

'What does it mean?' asked Gina, as they all looked inquiringly at Anu.

'It means "love of fellow animals and love of the wild". According to the book, it boils down to "love of life" – which, of course, is what conservation and environmental issues are about – we want to save our planet.'

She read out the passage, which talked about *biophilia*, and they found it quite fascinating, agreeing that it should be something they referred to on their website for the JEACs.

The time went surprisingly fast, and then from 4 p.m. onwards, they took it in turns to watch the waterhole. After an early supper at 5 o'clock, the boys had a quick nap for an hour and a half, while Anu and Gina took turns in watching the waterhole for any signs of movement by the men, but they did not see anything interesting.

Once the boys were awake, they dressed quickly, while Anu made everyone a cup of hot chocolate.

'Well, time to go out and follow Anu's plan,' said Rohan.

'Do we all know what we have to do?' asked Anu.

'Yes – sure,' chorused the others. Hunter would stay with the girls.

Suddenly Gina said, 'Listen, it's the peacocks calling.'

They all listened, and Rohan said grimly, 'Their weird call of "Helllp! Helllp!" is certainly appropriate at this time, isn't it?'

'I guess we'd better go and see how we can help them,' said Nimal, patting Hunter goodbye.

Rohan and Nimal left the cave and went into hiding so quietly, that Anu and Gina did not even spot them. The girls saw no signs of any men either, and though some peacocks came down to the waterhole, none of them were harmed. The night passed without incident.

The boys returned to the cave in the early hours of the morning. The girls were both awake and taking turns to keep watch, and by 4:30 a.m., four exhausted children, and one tired dog, fell asleep in the cave after a very scrappy breakfast.

Nimal was the first to wake up, around noon, and after a glance at the time, he roused the others.

'Well, what a wasted night,' said Anu gloomily. 'I'm sorry, folks. I did think those chaps would return to this waterhole, but maybe they went to another one – though we didn't hear any shots close by either.'

'Perhaps no peacocks went down to the other waterholes last night but stayed in their trees, too scared to come down at night,' said Rohan.

'Do you think we should give up the idea of lying in wait for the crooks?' asked Anu.

'Of course not,' said Rohan. 'We can't expect things to happen every single night, and we have to exercise a lot of patience when dealing with these types of matters. Your idea's a good one, sis.'

'I agree. We certainly shouldn't give up right now. Let's stick to it for at least a couple of nights,' added Nimal.

'Looks like rain tonight – there are some heavy black clouds hovering around,' said Rohan, peering out of the opening.

'That's good,' said Nimal, to everyone's surprise. He continued matter-of-factly, 'That means we may find trails of footprints if the ground is damp.'

'True,' said Rohan, 'and maybe we'll need the umbrella after all; but I think we should wear raincoats tonight.'

'Fortunately they're also dark green and black,' said Gina, 'so they won't be spotted easily.'

They sat down to a meal, and then after reading for a while, went to sleep again. Their alarms were set for 6:00 since the boys planned to be in position by 7:00 at the latest.

Rohan's alarm went off under his pillow and he was up in a jiffy.

'Time to wake up,' he said, prodding the others. 'We'll have a quick, light meal, and maybe we should take some sandwiches with us to our hideout. Gina, do you mind sitting at the entrance and keeping an eye on the waterhole right away?'

'No problemo, chief,' said Gina, dragging her sleeping bag to the entrance and grabbing her binoculars. 'Boy – it's definitely going to rain tonight – the sky's as black as anything.'

'Why don't you boys get dressed while I make the sandwiches,' said Anu. 'Also, don't forget to take everything you need.'

'Right,' said Nimal, hurriedly tidying his sleeping bag and pulling on his 'jungle kit', as they called the clothes his parents had sent them. 'I think we should take the umbrella, too, yaar,' he continued, 'since it'll actually be useful if it rains.'

'Sure, why not,' said Rohan.

He dressed in a jiffy and then ticked off on his checklist, the things they had to take with them. 'Let's see: we have one walkie-talkie; the umbrella; our raincoats and knapsacks; torches since it's pitch black outside; a flare and lighter if required; and we're wearing our jungle kits. Have I missed anything?'

'Sounds like you got it all, yaar,' said Nimal. He turned to the dog, 'Hunter, you stay here again and watch with the girls.'

Hunter whined softly in agreement. He was getting used to all this coming and going, and although he sensed that something strange was going on, he was content to be with his 'family', determined that no harm would come to them while he was on guard.

'Here are your sandwiches and drinks,' said Anu, handing over a bag to Nimal to put in his knapsack. 'I've also put in a few apples and a chocolate bar each.'

'Thanks, Anu,' said Rohan gratefully.

They sat down beside Gina, as she kept watch, and ate a meal. They all enjoyed their picnic style meals, and it was great to have the little stove and pans so that they could warm up some of the cold samosas and Chinese rolls that Vida and their mother had provided for them. Hunter had his own special food and, of course, the children always fed him titbits.

'Well, I guess we're ready to roll,' said Rohan, getting up and stretching. 'Let's go, yaar, and please grab the umbrella. I'll call you, girls, as soon as we're in position, so that you know we're set and, hopefully, you won't be able to see us.'

'Good luck, you two,' said the girls, and Hunter agreed with a tiny bark and a wag of his tail. He seemed to know when he had to be quiet.

The boys set off, and Anu cleared up, while Gina continued to keep watch.

Anu sat on her sleeping bag, at the back of the cave, so that her reading light would not shine out of the opening; Hunter cuddled up next to Gina.

'Do you want me to take over for a while, Gina?' asked Anu, a little later.

'Not just now, thanks,' said Gina. 'I don't mind keeping watch a bit longer. It seems to be getting even darker and there's not the teeniest breeze – I guess it's the calm before the storm. Do you think the animals will come down to the waterhole tonight if it rains heavily?'

'Oh, yes, they're sure to come,' replied Anu. 'In fact, they'll likely come in large groups tonight since they'll wait for the rain to ease off a bit and rush down to drink while it isn't pouring too heavily. Any signs of the men yet?'

'Nope,' said Gina. 'I'll let you know the minute I suspect anything.'

Anu settled down with a book. Ten minutes later her walkie-talkie beeped.

'Hello! Hello!' came Rohan's voice, over the machine. 'Do you read me, Anu and Gina? Over.'

Anu picked up her receiver, 'Hi, Rohan, I'm receiving you clearly. Are you in your bush already? Over.'

'Not yet,' said Rohan. 'We heard voices, not far from us, as we were coming to our spot. They didn't sound like any of the staff, so we hid in some thick undergrowth. Over.'

'Where are the voices now?' began Anu, and then stopped when Gina whispered urgently to her. 'Hang on a sec, Rohan,' she said hurriedly, 'I believe Gina's seen something.'

'I think the men are hiding in a bush, Anu,' whispered the little girl. 'There was a flash of lightning, just now, and I saw two figures fairly clearly.'

'Rohan,' said Anu softly over the walkie-talkie, 'stay where you are and don't make a sound. Gina thinks she's spotted the men near the waterhole – I'll call you in ten minutes, or so, with more information. Over and out.'

Anu doused the lantern, grabbed her binoculars, and moved over to lie beside Gina. The little girl was very excited and silently pointed towards where she had seen figures.

Anu looked carefully in the direction of Gina's pointing finger and then said quietly, 'You're absolutely right, kiddo. They're in that big bush on our right – two of them; and the skinny one's still wearing his red scarf.'

'The scarf made it more obvious,' whispered Gina. 'Also, they're not very good at moving quietly – in fact, they don't seem to think they need to be careful at all. They shook the bushes like crazy as they crawled in, and that's what gave them away in the first place.'

'Good work, hon,' said Anu, giving the little girl a hug. 'Let's wait for ten minutes so that they have time to settle down and we're sure they won't be moving again in a hurry, then I'll call the boys and tell them to be extra careful as they go into hiding themselves.'

The crooks seemed to have decided that they were quite safe from anyone catching them on an obviously dark and stormy night.

'Just look at the cheek of them,' muttered Gina angrily, a few minutes later. 'They're not in the least bit scared; they even have a torch, and are smoking and playing cards while they wait. Can you beat that?'

'I guess they feel really secure tonight,' said Anu. 'After all, they wouldn't dream that we were right up here, or that the boys are going to trail them later on. Well, I guess I can call Rohan now and tell him that this is the best time for them to hide in their bush. The men are unlikely to notice them, and the thunder helps cover any small noises.'

She picked up the walkie-talkie and called in. Rohan answered promptly and listened intently as she quickly updated him on the situation, telling him the precise location of where the men were hidden so that the boys could be extra cautious.

'Right! We're on our way,' murmured Rohan. 'Keep an eye on them though, and if they look suspiciously at our bush, signal me immediately – I have my earpiece in. Over and out.'

Gina agreed to keep a close watch on the men to see if they looked around suspiciously, while Anu would survey the rest of the area. Hunter nosed around them; he could not figure out where Rohan's voice was coming from, and kept sniffing at the walkie-talkie as if he thought Rohan was hiding in it.

'Hello, Anu,' said Rohan's voice, a little later. 'We're in place. Did you see us come in? Can you spot us now? Did the men look suspicious at anything? Over.'

'Hi, Rohan,' said Anu in surprise. 'Great work you two. I didn't see you get into place at all, and we can't see you now either. That strange-looking bush is a great hiding spot, and it sure is humongous. Your voice is quite faint, though, so, perhaps, cup your hand around the mouthpiece when you talk. Hang on a sec – I'll pass you on to Gina, who's watching the men.'

'Rohan,' whispered Gina, 'the men are still playing cards – they haven't stopped since we first saw them and have not even looked up – so they obviously don't have a clue that you chaps are around. Can you see where they are? It's kind of dark, but if you look carefully, you can just about spot them by the faint torchlight and the smoke rising from the bush. They're in the same bush we first saw them in, to our right and across from you. Over.'

'Let me just adjust my binocs, Gina – okay, Nimal's spotted the smoke, but we can't see the guys. I guess we're going to have some action tonight, for sure, even though I hope the peacocks stay away from this waterhole. Over,' said Rohan quietly.

'I'm glad things are coming to a head,' said Anu, when Gina handed back the walkie-talkie, 'but remember, try not to get too angry if they *do* kill a bird, and be careful when you follow them. I'll beep you over the walkie-talkie, as agreed, when they start moving. Well, good luck – we'll keep in touch regularly. Over and out.'

She and Gina both kept watch, but nothing more happened for a while. Gina fell asleep and Anu watched some deer and wild boar come down to the waterhole, followed by monkeys and a couple of jackals. An hour passed. Gina woke up, and looked out of the cave sleepily.

'Oh, oh, it's starting to rain,' said Gina, 'and that lightning's so brilliant.'

Anu agreed, 'Yes, it certainly lights up the whole area. Although I can see the men fairly clearly, I still can't see the boys in their hiding place. I wonder if I would be able to get a snapshot of the crooks at the next flash of lightning, or if it'll still be too dark. My zoom lens is pretty powerful.'

'Good idea,' said Gina eagerly. 'Why don't you try – and if you do get it that'll be great, and we'd have even more proof. You know, sis, I think those men are really stupid; even the bush they've picked to hide in is not very thick, and when there's a flash of lightning, I can see them quite clearly.'

'I guess the fact that they have guns, makes them feel safe,' said Anu, picking up her camera and fitting on the zoom lens.

She got everything ready and then settled down to wait for the next flash of lightning, which came a few minutes later, and she clicked away busily, taking three shots in that time.

'Wow! You certainly work fast with that camera,' said Gina in admiration. 'Do you think you got some clear shots?'

'I've a feeling at least one of them will be good,' said Anu. 'And the men looked up just as I clicked – but you never can tell till the pictures have been developed. I'll try for a few more to be on the safe side.'

She got a few more shots at the next flash of lightning, and then put down her camera and picked up her binoculars.

'Why don't you have a short nap, Gina?' she said. 'You've been yawning for the past while – I'll keep an eye on the waterhole. It's almost 2 a.m. now, and I think the rain'll keep the animals away for a bit.'

'I am a bit sleepy – but I don't want to miss anything,' admitted Gina. 'Also, the men have stopped playing cards, now that it's raining, and something may happen.'

'Don't worry. I'll wake you up if things start moving. In any case, the animals won't come down while it's raining so heavily,' said Anu.

'Could you wake me when it stops raining?' asked Gina, moving her sleeping bag away from the entrance so that Anu could lie there comfortably. 'I want to see which other animals come down to the water.'

'Okay,' said Anu. She looked at her watch and continued, 'I think it's time to check in with the boys to see how they're doing. The men don't seem to be bothered much by the rain, and they're still smoking. Sleep tight. I promise to wake you when the rain stops.'

Gina cuddled up with Hunter, who was yawning with boredom, and went to sleep almost immediately. Anu beeped the boys on the walkie-talkie.

'Hello, Rohan. Come in, please. Over.'

'Hi, Anu,' came Rohan's voice. 'Boy, is it ever pouring with rain. We're lucky to be under such a thick shelter – not a drop of water's reached us so far, though the trail's getting pretty damp. I guess that'll help us when we have to follow the chaps. Nimal's having a nap, and it looks like the men are still in the same spot. Anything new at your end? Over.'

'Nothing, other than I took a few shots with my camera when there was lightning and, hopefully, some of them will come out clearly. Gina's also asleep and I'm keeping watch. Do you think the birds will come down in the early hours of the morning? Over.'

'They'll have to, at some stage,' said Rohan. 'Perhaps the rain will ease in an hour or so – I'm going to stretch my legs, for five minutes, when Nimal wakes up, and will walk away from here. I'm getting pretty cramped, despite this bush being so large and comfy. I'll beep you if anything unusual happens. Over.'

'Right,' said Anu. 'I'm not going to keep constant watch till it stops raining, so please beep me when it does. Also, give me a second before you sign off – I'm going to move my lantern near the opening of the cave. Can you see any light from our cave? Over.'

'Nothing to be seen at all,' said Rohan. 'You're well hidden. Over and out.'

Anu switched off the walkie-talkie, keeping the earpiece on so that she could hear if Rohan beeped her, and settled down to finish her book. She had brought five books with her to the cave, and had already finished reading two of them. Every now and then she would take up her binoculars and check to see if the men were still there. They were – and did not move from their spot.

CHAPTER 13

The Wild Boar Trail

A few hours later the rain eased off. The early morning sounds of the jungle, awakening from a dark and wet night, surrounded the waterhole, and Anu prodded Gina gently.

'Gina! Gina, wake up, the rain's stopped,' said Anu. 'It's dawn and there are a few animals coming down to the water.'

Gina woke up and moved her sleeping bag close to the entrance again. She picked up her binoculars and looked out over the waterhole.

The sky was a soft, baby blue, with little white clouds floating lazily across, shot with tinges of orange. Birds and animals were coming down to the waterhole, chattering and grunting. Everything looked newly washed and extra bright, while the grass glimmered with raindrops and dew.

'Oh, wow!' exclaimed the little girl in excitement. 'Look at that family of wild boar and babies. There must be two families together because there are eight small fellows and three adults. Oh, aren't they sweet? Can you try to get a picture of them for me, Anu? Please.'

'Sure,' said Anu obligingly, picking up her camera. 'They're cute – I wonder why there are only three adults.'

She took a few shots of the boars, focusing especially on the piglets who were frolicking near the water, and then some more shots of the other animals that came down to the waterhole in batches. There were hundreds of birds, jackals, porcupine and many species of deer and antelope.

'Wouldn't it be funny if some of the animals sniffed out Nimal and went over to him?' said Gina. 'Remember last year when one baby piglet was injured and it was kept in the menagerie? It wanted to play with him and wouldn't let him alone – but it ran away if we came too close. He's so lucky.'

'He is, indeed, but I sure hope they don't do that today,' said Anu with a grin.

'Oh, here come the pheasants and partridges,' said Gina a while later. 'I wonder if the peacocks will come down, too. Oh, no! Look at the men, Anu. They've stopped playing cards and smoking, and have their guns in their hands.'

Anu put down her camera and picked up her binoculars. The men were watching the waterhole carefully, and each of them had a gun on his knee.

Gina quickly scanned the area around the waterhole, looking for signs of peacocks coming down – and she spotted six of them.

'Anu, quick, to your left, near the boys,' she gasped. 'The peacocks are coming to the water.'

The girls watched anxiously as the peacocks approached the waterhole cautiously, looking nervously around. A couple more birds flew down from a nearby tree to join the others at the waterhole.

'The boys must have seen the peacocks by now,' whispered Anu. She turned her binoculars on the men and groaned. 'Oh, no! The men are getting ready to shoot, and there's nothing we can do. Gina, cover your eyes.'

Gina immediately hid her face, while Anu watched in horror as both men took aim and fired at the beautiful birds. They each fired two shots in quick succession. The gunshots scattered the animals and birds away from the waterhole, and they all disappeared into the jungle except for three peacocks which lay dead on the ground.

The men ran to pick up the birds, put them in a bag, and then, passing close to where the boys were hidden, they went off into the jungle. They did not appear to be in any great hurry and slowly made their way up the trail, chatting as they went. Anu managed to get a few snapshots of them, including one clear picture of their faces.

Hunter barked at the noise of the shots, and was immediately shushed by Gina who was crying with anger and sorrow. He licked her face, not knowing what was happening other than realizing that his two friends in the cave were very upset and worried. They heard a couple of peacocks give their weird call for help again.

'And to think we can't even help them properly,' said Anu furiously, wiping away tears and pounding her fist into the sleeping bag in frustration.

She quickly beeped Rohan, 'Rohan, come in. Over. Not that the boys can't see the men take off,' she said to Gina as she waited for Rohan to answer. 'I just hope they won't do anything stupid, but will follow the men cautiously. Those men are real brutes. Where *are* the boys? There's no response.'

Impatiently she tried again with no luck. 'I'll give them five minutes and then try again,' she said to Gina.

Meanwhile, Rohan and Nimal had obviously seen everything, too, and both of them were hopping mad. Nimal placed a restraining hand on Rohan's shoulder in case he lost his temper and jumped out at the men. However, angry though he was, Rohan knew he would only endanger Nimal and himself, and possibly the girls, too, if he did anything foolish. So he curbed his temper. They waited till the men were out of sight before saying anything.

'I'd just love to go and punch those guys out,' exploded Rohan, grinding his teeth angrily.

'So would I,' groaned Nimal. He added impulsively, 'Why don't we try and knock them out now? After all, they don't know we're right behind them, and we could take them by surprise.'

'Tempting, but too dangerous, yaar – we don't really stand a chance against their guns,' said Rohan, who had regained his cool logic. 'We're better off sticking to our plan and following the crooks. I think they have enough of a lead by now – so let's go. I'll respond to Anu's beeps first – she's beeped several times.'

'Hi, Anu,' said Rohan. 'Come in. Over.'

'Rohan, I was getting worried,' said Anu. 'What's happening? Over.'

'Sorry, I didn't want to speak in case the crooks heard us, but we're going to follow them now. Don't worry, we'll be fine. Over and out.'

The boys set off cautiously, following the trail the men had taken, but keeping to the undergrowth. They did not see any footprints at first, since the canopy of trees was so thick in that particular area that no rain had seeped through.

'Oh, good, here are some footprints at last,' said Rohan, sometime later. 'We're going in the right direction at least. I don't hear any sounds from up ahead, Nimal – do you?'

'Nothing right now,' said Nimal, whose hearing was extremely acute, 'but I knew we were on the right trail since I could hear them chatting ahead of us, even though they were speaking very softly. It's a good thing this jungle has thinned out a bit and the rain was able to seep through and dampen the ground.'

'Maybe we'd better call the girls again,' said Rohan, 'and tell them where we are. I think we're fairly safe from being heard.'

'I'll do it, if you like,' said Nimal. He took the walkie-talkie from Rohan and beeped the girls. 'Hi there, Anu, come in, please. Over.'

'Hey, Nimal,' came Anu's voice over the machine. 'What's happening and where are you two? Over.'

'Well, we've just found some footprints on the trail and we're following them,' said Nimal. 'Are you two okay? Over.'

'Yes – other than the fact that we wish we could catch those crooks right now and hand them in to the police,' said Anu angrily. 'Keep in touch and don't let them see you. And, for goodness' sake, be careful. How's Rohan's temper? Over.'

'He's cool,' said Nimal. 'Don't worry, we'll be careful. Talk to you soon. Over and out.'

The boys continued to follow the footprints, which went along a trail they were familiar with.

'No more prints,' said Rohan, coming to a halt after they had tracked the men for nearly an hour. 'Let's split up and see if we can find them again. There are a lot of rocks around this area, so we may have to look for the prints beyond them – you search on that side of the trail and I'll search here. Perhaps we should call the girls again and let them know where we are. Also, since I think we've found the general direction in which the crooks' hideout is, we should ask them to get a hold of Dad and ask him to join us, with some of the staff, to help capture these chaps if we find them.'

'Good idea,' said Nimal. 'Maybe Gina could go home, with Hunter, while Anu holds the fort at the cave, with the walkie-talkie.'

Rohan called Anu and briefly updated her on the situation. 'We just followed the Wild Boar Trail, but now we're near those rocks and have lost track of the men. Over.'

'Can't we come and join you?' asked Anu, eagerly. 'You're having all the fun. Over.'

'Not just yet,' said Rohan, 'but if Gina can go with Hunter and get Dad and the others, collect you next, and you signal us, we'll tell you exactly where we are and you can all come down together and be in on the capture. For now, we need you two to organize things from that end, please. Over.'

'Okay, chief,' said Anu. 'Gina's awake and will set off immediately. Try and call me at 8:30 so I know that you're both safe. Over.'

'Will do, Anu. Good luck,' said Rohan. 'We'll continue our search in a few minutes. Over and out.'

Gina set off immediately with Hunter, and Anu sat in the cave, wishing she had something to do.

'I know,' she thought, 'I'll write down all that's happened so far. That'll not only keep me busy and give Peter some notes to read, but will also help with a story later on when I decide to write up this adventure.'

She settled down to her writing. An hour and a half later Gina and Hunter arrived back, both of them panting heavily.

'Gina! What's the matter? Why are you crying? Where are Dad and the others?' asked Anu, giving the little girl a glass of water and making her sit down.

'Anu, there's no one to be found,' said Gina desperately. 'I went home, and the house was deserted. Then I called Peter's place, and there was no one there either. I just got their answering machine. I don't know what's happened to all of them.'

Anu gazed at her in silence, her mind whirling with a confusion of thoughts. It did not make sense that none of the adults were around.

'Did you think of calling one of them on a mobile phone, or of calling Mike or the Mallicks from home to see if they were there?' asked Anu at last. The Mallicks were a young couple who also lived and worked on the Conservation and were an hour away from the Patels.

'Oh, gosh! No, I didn't think of that,' said Gina in dismay. 'I should've tried Mike's mobile. I just wanted to get back as soon as possible and see what you thought we should do next. Sorry.'

'Don't worry – I'd have done the same,' said Anu consolingly.

She thought hard, her brow furrowing in concentration while Gina and Hunter looked at her expectantly. Suddenly her face cleared, and she slapped her knee.

'I know where they are,' she said, looking at her watch which also showed the date. 'Today is the twentieth and remember Mum was talking about that big fundraising event in Hardwar to raise some money for the Conservation, and most people were going to it, leaving only a few staff behind to deal with emergencies? They were leaving early morning, around 5 o'clock, so that they had enough time to set up things. I think they were also preparing lunch for the crowd. I doubt they'll be back before 6:30 this evening.

'I guess they didn't expect us to discover anything so quickly, and therefore felt that a few staff could check up on us and also handle emergencies.'

'Just our luck,' groaned Gina. She got up and wandered around the cave restlessly. 'Now what should we do?'

'I think we'll wait to hear from the boys and then decide what our next plan of action should be,' said Anu sensibly. 'If we go off again to find the adults, we'll be out of range for the walkie-talkies, and the boys won't be able to get a hold of us. We're going to have to deal with this one ourselves, kiddo. So let's have a cup of hot chocolate and some breakfast while we wait to hear from them. They should call in about an hour.'

Anu didn't want Gina going off by herself again, as the little girl was obviously quite upset and she wanted to let her calm down.

Gina settled down a bit; Anu boiled some eggs and they ate a quick breakfast. Neither of them was very hungry, but Anu insisted that they eat a proper meal, knowing that they would need energy to deal with whatever cropped up.

'Let's pack our knapsacks so that we're all ready to go,' suggested Anu, who was anxious to keep Gina's mind off the terrible things that had happened. She also wanted to keep busy herself, to stop her imagination from running riot.

'Good idea,' said Gina. 'I only have my flute in mine just now, and I don't think I'll bother to remove it. But I'll take a torch, and wear my special clothes.'

'Great. We'll take some food and drink in case we have to be out for lunch – let's split the load. I'll also take my camera and change my clothes,' said Anu, 'and, of course, the walkie-talkie must come with us.'

She looked at her watch and continued, 'You know, it's 9:15 and the boys haven't beeped us yet. I wonder if I should call them.'

'Go ahead and try,' said Gina. She was eager for action.

Anu picked up the walkie-talkie and called in.

'Hello, hello, Rohan, Nimal, come in, please. Over.'

She waited for a response but received none. She tried again a couple of times but there was still no response. She began to look a bit worried, and tried yet again.

'Hello, Rohan, Nimal. This is Station A. Come in, please. Over.'

'No reply at all,' said Gina, biting her fingers nervously. 'I don't think you're even getting through. Maybe they've turned off the walkie-talkie. I think something has happened and we should go and look for them.'

Anu turned off her set, looking grim, and nodded in agreement.

'Okay, let's go, Gina,' she said. 'I think I'll also take along the small medical kit – just in case either of them has injured themselves. Boy, am I ever glad we have Hunter with us. Come on, Hunter, we're going to look for the boys and I don't know if they're all right.'

They set off cautiously. They were familiar with what the Conservation folk called the Wild Boar Trail, as it ended up at a big waterhole frequented by wild boar. There were also a few large rocks under some thick, prickly bushes, halfway along the trail.

CHAPTER 14

A Cosy Hideout

As for the boys, they were having an exciting time.

Before they continued their search, Rohan removed his earphone for the walkie-talkie – and put the unit in the smaller pocket of his knapsack so that he could reach it with ease. He turned the beeper on so that he or Nimal could hear it when the girls called.

They had split up to search for more footprints which could give them some indication of where the men had disappeared to. They searched among the brush, and off the trail.

'Nothing here,' called Nimal, after he had searched his side. 'Any luck your end?'

'No,' said Rohan slowly, 'but there's something funny about this rock. Come over here.'

Nimal hurried over to where Rohan was on his knees closely examining a gorse bush and the large flat rock near it. He looked at where Rohan was pointing.

'Do you see anything unusual about this rock?' asked Rohan eagerly, keeping his voice low.

'No,' began Nimal, and then paused. 'Actually, yeah – in the first place it's unusually clean and, secondly, there's a large smooth spot to the right of it which looks as if it could have been made by this rock being moved to that position and then back to its original spot.'

'Not only that,' said Rohan in tones of suppressed excitement, 'but there's half a footprint on the left side of the rock, and the imprint of the bag again. I think there's something fishy about this rock. Maybe there's an underground cavern or something below.'

'But how do we get it open?' asked Nimal, his eyes gleaming in anticipation of more adventure.

'Look for some kind of a lever,' said Rohan, 'it may be under one of the smaller rocks around here.'

The boys searched the area thoroughly and then Nimal gave a low cry. 'Look here, Rohan! Quick.'

Rohan rushed over to where Nimal was crouched over a small hole made by a rock, which had been moved away to the side. Nestled in the hole was a lever, cunningly set so that it would be hard to find unless you knew what you were looking for.

The boys high-fived each other gleefully.

'Shall we open it and see what's underneath?' asked Nimal eagerly.

'Of course,' said Rohan.

Nimal pulled the lever, which moved easily, sliding the rock silently to the right and exposing a large round hole. The sun lit up the aperture, which looked as if it dropped down about one and a half metres.

The boys peered into the hole – there did not appear to be any sign of the men. Quietly, they dropped down into the opening.

'How does this close from inside?' whispered Nimal. 'After all, they must have closed it behind them.'

'I'm looking for another lever,' said Rohan softly, groping around the roof of the tunnel. 'Aha, here it is.' He quickly closed the aperture and they were left in utter darkness.

'Put your torch on, but shield it with your hand,' whispered Rohan, 'and then walk behind me. That way we'll both have enough light to find our way, but it won't be bright enough to be seen by anyone who may be looking in our direction. It looks as though there's a tunnel ahead – let's go.'

Tense with excitement and treading softly, the boys followed the passageway which, though quite narrow, was high enough for Rohan to be able to walk erect. As they rounded a bend in the tunnel, Rohan came to an abrupt stop, and Nimal bumped into him.

'What's up? Why've you stopped?' whispered Nimal.

'There's a light ahead of us,' murmured Rohan. 'Switch off the torch.'

Nimal obeyed immediately, and both boys crept forward silently. The light got brighter and soon they were gazing into a large underground cavern that opened before them. It was formed of rock and had a sandy floor. Two large lanterns lit the area fairly well.

There were two men sitting on the floor, fortunately with their backs to the boys, and they were pulling the feathers off the peacocks they had killed. They were obviously not afraid of being caught; they had a radio playing and were smoking and talking quite loudly. They felt quite safe in their cosy little hideout.

Spread out in the cavern were two sleeping bags; two bags with round bottoms – one of which the men used for putting the birds in when they killed them if they did not have time to pluck the feathers at the site of the kill, and the other bag for the feathers; there was also a transmitter and cans of food. A little spring ran down the wall opposite to where the boys were hiding and flowed into a stream which ran under the rocks and probably came out somewhere in the jungle.

As the boys watched, the men finished their job, threw the shorn birds into a bag, washed their hands in the stream and began opening cans of food. Rohan and Nimal listened intently to the conversation.

'Well, Pradeep,' said the man in the yellow shirt, tucking into his food, 'we have a good haul now and maybe we should call up the boss and tell him to come and pick this lot up tomorrow night. I'm sure we can get some more during the next few weeks.'

'I guess so,' replied Pradeep slowly, 'but I'm getting a bit worried about staying here much longer, Chand. I think we've been here too long already, and though no one has caught us or knows where we disappear to, our luck could run out at any time.'

'Oh, quit being so nervous,' said Chand impatiently. 'You're scared just because those men saw us that night, but we dealt with them promptly. Also, who would ever guess that there's a hideout like this? We're perfectly safe, yaar. And when we're ready to go, all we have to do is contact the boss and ask him to come, in his chopper, and haul us up one night.'

'But you know those kids we saw that night,' began Pradeep anxiously, 'what if they spot us? They seem to wander about the jungle quite a bit.'

He stopped as Chand snorted in disgust. 'Even if those kids saw us and found our hiding place, we're grown men and a match for any kids. I wouldn't worry about them at all. What? Are you scared of a bunch of stupid kids?' asked Chand scathingly.

He finished his meal, pulled out his sleeping bag and lay down on it. 'Just relax and go to sleep, yaar,' he continued, 'I'm totally exhausted – it was a long, wet night.'

Pradeep grimaced and switched off the radio. Turning off one lantern, he lay down on his sleeping bag, too.

The boys looked at each other and then Rohan signalled Nimal to go back along the tunnel so that they could decide on a plan of action.

Just as they turned, their walkie-talkie beeped. It sounded very loud in the quiet cavern, and even though Rohan put his hand in his knapsack and turned it off immediately, both men heard it and were up in a jiffy, racing towards the sound.

'Run, Nimal, quick!' yelled Rohan, turning and sprinting towards the exit, with Nimal just in front of him.

'Stop or I'll shoot,' yelled Chand angrily. 'I don't care who you are – but I mean it. Stop and turn around with your hands in the air.'

His voice was extremely threatening, and Rohan immediately called out, 'Nimal, hold it! This chap's dangerous.'

Both boys came to a halt and turned slowly to meet the men who came running up, their guns in hand, and flashing torches into the dark tunnel.

'I told you those kids would be around,' whined Pradeep, 'and now they'll give away the whole show.'

'Shut up, man,' snarled Chand. He turned to the boys who had their hands up and signalled them to move into the cavern ahead of him. The boys went slowly back and stood in the middle of the cavern.

'Okay,' said Chand, glaring at them, 'who are you and what are you doing here? How did you find us? Who else knows that you're here?'

The boys said nothing.

Chand turned to Pradeep and said, 'Check them out and see what made that noise.'

Just then Rohan's watch beeped 9:30 a.m. It sounded like the walkie-talkie and the men looked at each other in relief. 'It's just a stupid watch,' said Chand, 'don't bother to check the knapsacks, Pradeep.'

So the girls at least would not be discovered, thought Rohan thankfully.

Chand threatened the boys at gunpoint and asked the same questions again. This time Rohan, after a quick glance at Nimal, elected to answer.

'We live on the Conservation and are home for the summer holidays. We were just playing in the jungle when we saw the rock, found the lever and came in to see where the tunnel led to. We had barely come in when my watch beeped.' He continued angrily, 'But we've heard of you and know that you're killing the peacocks.'

'That's none of your business,' said Chand nastily, 'and in any case, what do you think you kids are going to do about it? Now, shut up and I'll do the talking. Where are the two girls who were with you a few days ago?'

'Our parents and all the staff have gone away to some fundraising seminar or the other, and our sisters went too,' lied Nimal promptly. 'They didn't want to leave the girls behind.'

'Good,' said Chand, 'and for how long are they away?'

'Three days,' said Rohan, hoping that would make the men feel safe and, as a result, commit some careless mistakes.

'So no one knows that you're here and they won't miss you till they return,' said Chand, smiling grimly. 'Good! Well, for being nosy parkers, you're both going to be tied up while we finish our business here, and by the time you're found, we'll be far away. We'll leave an anonymous note for your parents so that they know where to look for you. We aren't murderers, after all.'

Chuckling nastily at what he considered to be a great joke, he and Pradeep tied the boys up securely, putting ropes about their ankles and also tying their hands behind their backs. They put them in a corner with their backs against the wall of the cavern and threw their knapsacks and the umbrella beside them. Then they lay down again and promptly went to sleep. Soon loud snores vibrated around the cavern.

Rohan and Nimal struggled with their bonds for a while and then gave up.

'Try and get some sleep, Nimal,' whispered Rohan. 'We'll need all our strength for later on and there's nothing we can do just now.'

Nimal nodded in agreement and they both slept fitfully. Rohan woke up to hear Chand on the transmitter. He listened without opening his eyes.

'54050, come in, please. This is 23060 calling,' said Chand.

There was a crackling over the air, and then another voice was heard. 'This is 54050, what do you want?'

'We're having a spot of trouble,' said Chand, 'nothing major that we can't handle, but it means that we need to get out of here tonight at midnight. Can you arrange this?'

'Okay,' responded the voice, 'but the boss won't be too happy. He still needs at least 400 more long feathers for his shipment. Have you got any more birds?'

'Yes, of course,' said Chand impatiently, 'and we're going out again tonight to get some more. I've just heard that everyone is away on some seminar or the other for a couple of days, so we can do a good round of the waterholes and then come to the pickup spot at midnight. Also, tell the boss to turn the helicopter lights off when it's hovering over the area to pick us up. Last time we could have been seen dropping over the wall if the guard in the tower happened to be looking our way.'

'Okay, will do. Over and out,' said the voice as it crackled off the transmitter.

'Chand, you'll have to tell me exactly where the pickup spot is,' said Pradeep anxiously. 'I'm not sure of my way in the jungle, like you are. If we're going to separate waterholes for the birds tonight, we may not be able to meet to go to the pickup spot together.'

Chand looked across at the boys, but Nimal was snoring lightly and Rohan kept his eyes closed and breathed deeply, pretending to be asleep. However, Chand was not willing to take any chances.

'I'll tell you on the way out,' he said, 'but in the meantime, let's discuss the other plans.'

He looked over at the boys again but they both appeared to be fast asleep. Then, feeling that even if they did wake up it would not really matter if the boys heard some of their plans as they could not free themselves of the ropes, Chand and Pradeep discussed which waterholes they would visit that evening. Each of them would visit three waterholes, which were frequented by peacocks and other animals and birds. The waterholes that Chand would go to were fairly far away from their hideout, but he would still have enough time to get back to the cave, pick up his things and then get out of the place. Rohan listened intently as the men finalized their plans. After their discussion, the men went to sleep again.

Rohan stayed awake for a while, racking his brains to think of ways in which they could escape. He was just wondering what the time was and thinking of how worried the girls would be, when his watch beeped 2 p.m. Nimal woke up, looked puzzled for a minute and then realized where they were. He glanced across at the men who were both snoring loudly, and then looked at Rohan.

'What do you think the girls are doing?' he asked softly.

'I wish I knew,' said Rohan. 'They must be worried sick by now. I just hope they don't come here and run into the men.'

'Perhaps they'll go home and try to get some help,' said Nimal.

'Let's hope so,' said Rohan.

Both boys fell silent as Chand rolled over and opened an eye. He looked at his watch and then prodded Pradeep.

'Wake up,' he said, 'and let's get some food. I suppose we should give these two kids something to eat, too.'

They opened some cans of food, ate their fill and then untied the boys' hands and gave them some food and water. Once the boys had eaten, their hands were tied again. The men played a game of cards for an hour or so and then went back to sleep. Rohan and Nimal had nothing to do and since they could not talk to each other freely, they, too, went to sleep.

Around 5:30 p.m. the men woke up, ate another meal, gave the boys some food, and then got ready to go out into the jungle to shoot more birds.

'What about our stuff here?' asked Pradeep. 'Shouldn't we get it ready so that we can move out quickly tonight?'

'Oh, we'll have plenty of time when we come back,' said Chand. 'In any case, you take your stuff when you get back and I'll collect mine when I return. I'll take the transmitter with my things, so it doesn't really matter that we'll be getting here at different times. Just collect your bags and get to the pickup spot.'

'Okay,' grunted Pradeep. He still did not seem too happy about the situation, but was obviously afraid of Chand.

Just as the men were ready to leave, they heard a muffled bark and then the patter of feet running down the tunnel. Both men froze, their guns in hand. The boys looked at each other in dismay as everyone turned towards the mouth of the tunnel. What on earth was happening now?

CHAPTER 15

Anu, Gina and Hunter Go Tracking

Meanwhile, the girls had had a fruitless search. They followed the wild boar trail and footprints to the rocks. When the footprints came to an end, they searched all over in an attempt to pick up the trail the boys had taken, but did not have any luck. They did not find the mark made by the bag near the rock, since the boys had smudged it with their shoes in the excitement of finding the lever.

Hunter was having a great time. He thought they were playing a fantastic game and would wander off into the bushes trying to burrow into what he thought were rabbit holes in the hopes of conversing with a sleeping bunny.

After searching for hours, in a wide area near the last footprint, the girls gave up. They had taken brief breaks in-between searches, but it was now past 3 p.m. and they were exhausted and frustrated. They had tried, unsuccessfully, to contact the boys on the walkie-talkie at regular intervals.

'Where on earth could the boys have got to, Gina?' asked Anu anxiously, sitting down on a tree stump.

Gina shrugged and slumped down on a rock. Hunter lay down beside her, his tongue lolling out.

'He looks thirsty,' said Gina, patting the dog, 'and we're out of water.'

'Okay, well, let's go back to the cave and think of a plan of action,' said Anu, getting up.

So they trudged wearily back to the cave and had hot soup and sandwiches. They gave Hunter some water and fed him, and then considered what they should do next.

'Maybe we should try the walkie-talkie again,' said Gina hopefully.

'I've a feeling something has made the boys turn it off,' said Anu thoughtfully. 'We've tried so many, many times, and they haven't responded. So either it's turned off or perhaps they found the hideout and have been captured by the men.'

'Oh, no!' exclaimed Gina. 'What do we do now, Anu? Mum and Dad won't be back till this evening, and we don't even know *where* the boys are, to even try and rescue them.'

'I was wondering if we should go back to the house and call Mike or the Mallicks on their mobile phones and ask them to get some of the staff who are still here, and perhaps some of the folk from the CH, to help us look for the boys,' said Anu. 'But I'm also worried that by the time we contact anyone, they get over here, and we bring them up to date on what has happened so far, the boys will be in more danger than ever – the delay might complicate things further. No, we need to think of another option.'

Gina nodded in agreement, and both girls pondered the situation in silence as they finished up their meal.

Hunter, meanwhile, was also wondering where Nimal and Rohan were. He missed them. So he picked up one of Nimal's socks, which happened to be bright blue, and brought it over to Anu. He dropped it at her feet and barked softly as if to say, 'Where is the boy this sock belongs to?'

Anu patted him absently and said, 'I don't know where they are, Hunter, but I sure hope we can find them soon.'

'Why don't we put Hunter on their trail?' asked Gina suddenly.

Anu stared at her. 'I mean,' continued Gina excitedly, 'we could show Hunter this sock of Nimal's and then say "Hunter, find Nimal". I know he's clever enough to understand what we're saying.'

'What a great idea, Gina,' said Anu, giving the little girl a hug.

She picked up the sock and pulled Hunter towards her. 'Now boy,' she said to the dog who was watching her intently, 'See this sock? You know it belongs to Nimal. Find him. Let's go and look for him and Rohan.'

Hunter gave a small whine as if he understood exactly what Anu was saying, and immediately set off down the tunnel to the entrance of their cave, looking back to see if the girls were following him.

The girls quickly stuffed some water and chocolate bars in their knapsacks and hurried after the dog, making sure they covered the entrance carefully behind them.

Hunter took them along the trail they had followed earlier and led them straight to the last footprint. Then he went over to the flat rock and stood by it, looking up at the girls.

'Okay, boy,' said Anu, patting the dog, 'you've done a great job so far, but what do you expect us to do here? This is just a large rock and, remember, we checked around it earlier?'

Hunter barked and then sniffed his way over to the smaller rock and the hole in which Nimal had found the lever. He pawed the hole, looked back at the girls, and whined.

The girls went over to him and Anu bent down to look into the hole. She saw the lever and turned to Gina in excitement.

'Gina, see what Hunter's found!' she exclaimed. 'This must be what the boys discovered, too. Shall we pull it and see what happens?'

'Of course,' said Gina, her eyes shining. She hugged Hunter, 'What a clever dog you are, Hunter – we'd never have found this lever if not for you.'

Anu tugged at the lever and the rock moved away silently, disclosing the opening the boys had found earlier that day. The girls looked at each other in excitement, and Hunter whined softly as he peered down the hole. He could tell that Nimal and Rohan had been there some time ago. Then, before the girls could say anything more, the dog leapt down into the hole.

'Oh, boy! Let's follow him quickly, Gina,' said Anu. 'I'll get down first and help you.'

'I'm fine, thanks,' said Gina, who was a gymnast.

They jumped in and heard Hunter running down the passage and then his loud, angry barking. They rushed down the tunnel, too, and heard Nimal's voice raised commandingly.

'Hunter, back boy! Hunter, sit! Don't shoot him, please,' pleaded the boy. 'He'll obey me.'

The girls saw the bright light at the mouth of the tunnel and peered in. They saw the two men with their guns pointed at Hunter. The dog, obedient to Nimal's command, was seated, but continued to snarl angrily at the men. They also saw the boys who were tied up and looking anxiously over at Hunter, hoping that he would not move.

Anxious for their dog, the girls ran into the cavern, and the boys groaned in unison as their last hope for help disappeared.

Gina promptly rushed over to Hunter and put her arms around him.

'You can't shoot our dog,' said the little girl defiantly, looking up at the men.

'So,' said Chand to the boys with a horrid smile, 'you were lying when you said your sisters were not here, weren't you? Well, you get what you deserve and we're going to tie *all* of you up, and,' he continued as Hunter growled menacingly, 'if you don't control that dog, I'll shoot him.'

'H-he w-w-will listen to us,' said Gina, her voice wobbling in fear. 'Y-you c-c-can see that he is obeying us even n-n-now.'

Anu went over to join Gina, and led her and Hunter over to where the boys were. She made Hunter sit down next to Nimal and Rohan, and she and Gina sat down as well. The dog licked the boys in greeting, but still growled as he kept an eye on the men.

Chand and Pradeep tied up the girls. Hunter reluctantly obeyed Nimal who was very stern when he told him to sit. The boys were furious that the girls were being treated roughly and tied up, but there was nothing they could do at present. They just tried to keep Hunter calm as they were all worried that he would attack the men who would then shoot him. Neither man appeared to want to get too close to Hunter.

Chand questioned the girls further. 'What on earth are kids like you doing, wandering around the jungle all by yourselves?'

'We were just playing hide-and-seek with our brothers,' said Anu, letting her imagination run riot, 'and then we totally lost the boys. We had agreed that if we couldn't find each other in a couple of hours, we would all meet back at the house. But my sister and I got there and the boys didn't come. So we came looking for them, and our dog got on the trail and followed them to this spot.'

The boys and Gina looked at Anu admiringly – she sure was quick at thinking up stories.

'But where are your parents and the other staff members?' asked Chand. 'Your brothers lied to us and said all of you had gone away.'

'They've gone to a function in Hardwar – it's a fundraiser for the Conservation,' said Anu.

'How do I know you're telling me the truth?' asked Chand. 'And, no, don't you boys try to intervene,' he continued, as Rohan tried to answer for Anu.

'Please,' said Anu, thinking fast again, and this time pretending to be very scared, 'you *have* to believe me. If I wasn't telling you the truth, do you really think that we'd have been so foolish as to come and look for the boys on our own, especially with my little sister who's so frightened already? We'd have brought the adults with us. After all, we're just two girls, and our parents would never have let us come by ourselves if they thought there was any danger. We had no choice. We knew we'd be on our own unless we were able to find our brothers – we were worried that they might have been injured in some way or the other.'

Gina started to cry, burying her head in Hunter's neck. Hunter whined and licked her cheek. He felt bad that the little girl was so unhappy.

'Okay! Okay!' said Chand hastily, 'for goodness' sake, stop crying.'

He believed Anu's story since he could not imagine that two girls would be so independent as to go wandering around the jungle on their own.

The men left the children alone and sat down a bit further off to discuss the situation.

'What do we do now?' asked Pradeep. 'The situation's getting worse. We'll be accused of kidnapping children, too, if we're caught.' He was close to panicking.

'Don't be so stupid, yaar,' said Chand impatiently, 'you're such a wimp. All we have to do is get the phone number for their parents, and once we're out of here, we'll get the boss to call and leave a message on their answering machine telling them where to find the kids. In any case, it's only a matter of a few hours more. So quit your complaining.'

However, it was obvious that he, too, was rattled. He thought for a few moments, and then turned to Rohan and demanded the telephone number for the main Conservation office. Rohan gave it to him.

'I think we'll make a slight change in plans,' said Chand to Pradeep. 'I'll take all my gear with me when I go, and leave it close to one of the waterholes – I'll pick it up on the way out. You can collect your things and the transmitter when you've finished since the waterholes you'll be covering are closer to this hideout than the ones I'm going to.'

'What about all the stuff here, and the kids?' asked Pradeep.

'Leave the foodstuff. Just collect your things, call the boss to update him on what's been happening and then pack only the transmitter and make for the pickup spot. We'll deal with the kids by calling their parents, as I said earlier. They won't come to any harm here, and a few hours of starvation should teach them a lesson not to interfere in adult doings. Hurry up; we should leave by 7 o'clock.'

Both men started collecting their things and putting them in two large sacks so that everything was ready for a fast getaway. Then Chand took his sack, they both picked up their guns and left the underground hideout without another word to the children.

CHAPTER 16

The Umbrella

The men went up the tunnel and then there was silence.

'Hunter,' said Nimal, after a few minutes, 'go find the men.'

Hunter got up and ran down the passage. However, he did not bark and just came back to lick Nimal and the others.

'I guess they've gone,' said Rohan, with a sigh of relief. 'Thank goodness!'

'How come you boys got caught?' asked Anu, trying, unsuccessfully, to find a comfortable spot on the ground.

The boys told their story, and then the girls reported on what had been happening to them.

'After all, we're just two girls,' mimicked Nimal, suddenly remembering Anu's act. 'You should be on stage, Anu. Even I – for a misguided moment – thought you were really scared.'

'Oh, well – if my writing doesn't prove lucrative, perhaps I *will* go on stage,' chuckled Anu. 'Good thing you remembered the fundraising event, Nimal.'

'I didn't,' said Nimal with a grin, 'I just made that up. Your wild imagination's infectious.'

'So, what do we do now?' asked Gina, who was very relieved that the whole group was back together.

'I wish I knew, kiddo,' said Rohan, 'but at the moment my brain seems to be dead. I can't help thinking of those horrible men out there, killing more peacocks and then escaping, when we know exactly what their plans are. And here we are, tied hand and foot, with no way of contacting any of the adults.' He banged his feet on the ground in frustration.

'If only we could get free,' said Nimal wistfully. 'Hunter, old boy, couldn't you pull out the Swiss army knife in my pocket and cut the ropes binding us? I'm sure you're clever enough for that.'

'Oh, my hat! The umbrella!' yelled Rohan excitedly. 'How could I have forgotten it?'

He and Nimal beamed at each other while the girls stared at them as if they had gone mad.

'What about the ...' began Anu, when Nimal cut in.

'Of course! We're as good as free.'

The girls looked at the boys who were now grinning from ear to ear. 'Okay, let us into the secret, guys,' said Anu.

'We'll *show* you,' said Rohan with a laugh. 'Nimal, do you think you can get Hunter to pick up the umbrella and bring it to us? It's over there, in the corner with the knapsacks.'

'Hunter,' said Nimal, 'fetch the umbrella.' He nodded his head towards the corner.

Hunter looked at Nimal with his head on one side. He knew Nimal wanted him to fetch something from that corner. He went over and pulled at Rohan's knapsack and dragged it over to Nimal.

'Not that one, old boy,' said Nimal patiently. 'The other thing.'

Hunter went over to the corner again. He sniffed at Nimal's knapsack this time and then looked over at Nimal inquiringly. When Nimal shook his head and repeated 'umbrella', the intelligent dog picked up the umbrella and brought it over to Nimal.

'Good dog,' said everyone, and Hunter wagged his tail, pleased that all the children were happy with him, but he could not understand why none of them petted him.

'Now, Anu,' said Rohan, 'call Hunter to sit near you so he doesn't get in the way. Nimal, turn around so that the umbrella is behind you and you can get your hands to the button.'

Anu called to Hunter who obediently went over to where the girls were seated and sat down next to them, giving them each a quick lick.

Nimal turned, grabbed the umbrella, and looked over his shoulder to make sure he got his finger on the right button. 'And, *voilà!*' he said, pressing the second button, which had been covered with tape. Immediately a sharp knife popped out of the parrot's beak and the girls gasped in amazement. Nimal held the knife firmly as Rohan struggled around so that his hands were close to the knife. Very carefully Rohan began to rub the ropes tying his hands together against the sharp edge of the knife.

'No wonder you two were so keen on bringing that umbrella,' said Anu. 'It sure has rescued us.'

Working steadily Rohan cut the ropes and was soon free. He quickly sliced through the rope around his feet, and then set Nimal free. Nimal took out his Swiss Army knife and between the two of them they released the girls as well.

They all patted and hugged Hunter who was overjoyed that they were no longer sitting in that strange position and unable to pet him. Of course, Rohan and Nimal had to explain about the umbrella to the girls, and they were all grateful that Rohan's pal had given him such a wonderful gift.

'What do we do now?' asked Anu anxiously. 'The men will get away if we don't hurry.'

'We have a bit of time,' said Rohan. 'We know that the pickup time is midnight. Pradeep is unlikely to come back here before 11 p.m. and it's only 7:30 now. Let's have something to eat and discuss what we should do next.'

'Great idea,' said Nimal. 'I'm starving and there are heaps of cans here, and a gas stove, too. Those crooks certainly didn't stint themselves in the food line.'

They set about getting together a quick meal and something to drink. Hunter was given a whole can of luncheon meat and biscuits for himself, as a reward for being so clever.

As they ate, they discussed the next steps.

'Anu, I think you and Gina should go straight home, and if there's no one home yet from the fundraiser, call Peter's place, Mike, the Mallicks or Dad on the mobile and get some help,' said Rohan. 'And, Anu – do whatever's necessary to get someone. You know there's a list of everyone's mobiles and phone numbers in the kitchen. We really need help at this stage.'

'Should we bring them back here?' asked Anu.

'I'm not sure about that,' said Rohan thoughtfully. 'The problem is that we don't know where the pickup spot is, or it would've been good if you could have taken the adults there to catch the other crooks.'

'What are you and Nimal going to do?' asked Gina curiously.

The boys looked at one another, and then Rohan said, 'I think Nimal will agree with me when I suggest that he, Hunter and I go after Pradeep and try to snare him. He seems to be extremely nervous, and I think we should be able to scare him into dropping his gun. Then we can grab him.'

Nimal nodded. 'Just what I was thinking, yaar. I can't bear the idea of them killing any more peacocks.'

'I know how you boys feel,' said Anu slowly, 'but are you sure it's not too dangerous? Shouldn't you wait for the adults to join you?'

'And he has a gun,' said Gina, looking scared. 'What if he shoots you?'

'Don't worry, Gina,' said Rohan, giving his little sister a hug. 'I have a plan and I think we can frighten him into thinking that we have a gun, too.'

'The umbrella, of course,' said Nimal. 'In the dark he'll be unable to see that it's merely an umbrella.'

'Exactimo,' said Rohan with a grin, 'and with Hunter to jump on him from behind and two hulking, athletic chaps like Nimal and me to hold him down, I don't think we'll have any problems at all. By the way, Nimal, grab some of that rope in the corner over there, and get me a few lengths, too. I think it'll come in handy.'

Nimal went over and cut a number of lengths of rope with his knife; as the boys each tied lengths of rope around their waists, Rohan continued. 'You know, Nimal, perhaps we can persuade Pradeep to tell us where the pickup point is.'

'That's a super duper idea, yaar,' said Nimal with a broad grin. 'I'm sure the three of us can get the info out of him. Ve vill find vays of making him tok, no?' he concluded, mimicking a comedian he had seen in a movie, and making the others laugh.

'And you can then contact us on the walkie-talkie and update us with current information, so that we can tell the adults where the pickup is located, and they can catch the crooks there,' said Anu.

'Yes,' said Nimal. 'Also, have someone contact the police and ask them to come over to the Conservation as soon as possible.'

'I also think we should take their transmitter with us,' said Anu, 'so that nobody can radio any problems to the boss if the crooks escape and manage to get back here.'

'Good idea,' said Nimal.

'I wonder why they use a transmitter instead of a mobile phone,' said Anu.

'Probably because it's not as easy to trace compared to a mobile number,' said Rohan. 'You can build illegal transmitters, but you *have* to get a phone number from the telephone service providers.'

'Hmmm, good point, Rohan,' said Anu. 'I never thought of that. Also, I guess, they wouldn't be able to charge a mobile out in the jungle.'

'Now, Anu and Gina,' said Nimal, 'don't forget that the pickup time for the crooks is midnight, so try and get everything organized as soon as possible at your end, so that things are in place by 11:30 at the latest.'

'And don't worry, girls,' added Rohan, seeing that Anu was looking a bit apprehensive but not wanting to say anything to frighten Gina. 'We won't do anything foolish and, if we're in major trouble, we'll set off a flare. Don't forget we also have Hunter to protect us and warn us of any danger – and,' he concluded, grimacing at her, 'I *promise* not to lose my temper and do anything foolish.'

'My biggest worry,' said Anu with a grin. 'Okay – then, once we get the adults, I guess we should set out on the main trail towards the waterhole where Chand may be, unless we hear from you as to where the pickup spot is – and in that event, we'll head there.'

'Makes sense,' said Rohan. 'Hopefully, by the time you reach the bungalow, we'd have caught Pradeep and got the info out of him to pass on to you.'

Everyone picked up their knapsacks, Anu put the transmitter into her bag and Nimal grabbed the umbrella. Anu and Rohan also took out the walkie-talkies and put in the earpieces.

'Well, good luck, boys,' chorused the girls. 'We'll get help as soon as we can,' continued Anu, 'and we'll be waiting for your call to tell us what the next steps are and where to meet.'

They set off down the tunnel to the exit. It was 8 p.m. Rohan moved the lever that opened up the hole and everyone clambered out, Rohan lifting Hunter so that the dog could leap out, too.

'Keep to the main trail,' whispered Rohan to the girls, as they waved goodbye.

The girls set off in one direction while the boys, who knew the exact location of the first waterhole Pradeep was going to, set off quietly in another direction, Nimal and Hunter leading the way this time.

CHAPTER 17

Pradeep in Trouble

'Here we are, Rohan,' said Nimal, stopping suddenly. 'Should we scout around and see if he's already finished with this waterhole? I don't hear or see a single animal, and it's possible that he's already moved on to the second waterhole.'

'Okay,' agreed Rohan softly, 'but since this chap has a gun, let's go together and Hunter is sure to sniff out anyone around here and warn us.'

They walked around the waterhole cautiously, using their binoculars to look for any signs of Pradeep. Hunter sniffed around, but did not growl. As the boys completed a circle of the waterhole, Rohan moved out of the undergrowth, and went towards the water, signalling to Nimal to stay behind with Hunter just in case Pradeep jumped out of the shrubbery. However, no one accosted him, and after a couple of minutes, Nimal and Hunter joined Rohan and they searched the area just near the water where the soil was damp.

'Look, he's been here all right,' said Rohan, pointing to a set of footprints. He and Nimal followed the prints and saw the spot where Pradeep must have squatted to pick up a bird. There was blood on a rock near the water.

'He got another bird,' said Nimal through his teeth. 'I guess we didn't hear the gunshots since we were in the underground cave.'

Angrily the boys examined the spot and then agreed to move on to the next waterhole.

'I think we should go really carefully,' cautioned Rohan, 'as it's most likely he'll be at the next waterhole.'

'Yeah,' agreed Nimal. 'How do you think we should try and grab him? Wait till he's killed a bird and comes out to get it, at which point his gun will be unloaded, or try and catch him before he kills another bird?'

'Well, ideally it would be better to prevent him killing a bird,' said Rohan hesitantly, 'but we really do need his gun to be unloaded before we can threaten him with our umbrella and Hunter knocks him down.'

'Okay, then, you carry the umbrella and I'll control Hunter so that he doesn't do anything before we're ready to jump the chap,' said Nimal.

'Right, and also, don't forget he has two shots in his gun,' said Rohan, taking the umbrella from Nimal. 'Let's go!'

They set off again, this time walking even more cautiously than before, since they were almost positive that Pradeep would be at the next waterhole. Nimal talked to Hunter in a low voice telling him not to make a sound and the dog was incredibly silent in his movements – not even a twig snapped under his paws.

They reached the undergrowth near the waterhole and scanned the area with their binoculars, looking for any hint of red since Pradeep had been wearing his red scarf when he left the hideout. They felt that the men would not be too cautious since they had left the children tied up in their hideout and they thought there were no adults around.

As they moved a bit further left, Hunter suddenly growled softly, and the boys stopped immediately, Nimal putting his hand on Hunter's collar to silence him. They scanned the area again, and then Nimal clutched Rohan's arm in excitement. When Rohan looked at him, he pointed to their left. About 300 metres away, there was a spiral of smoke coming out of a bush; focusing his binoculars on the smoke, Rohan scanned the bush and spotted Pradeep's red scarf.

There were no animals at the waterhole yet, so the boys moved away, made their plans in low tones, and then Nimal, after cautioning Hunter again, moved silently to a place closer to Pradeep, but behind him. He kept free of bushes since he wanted to be able to set Hunter on Pradeep as soon as Rohan threatened the man, and also be able to run out fast, himself. Hunter did not even growl.

Rohan also moved nearer Pradeep and quietly got in position behind a thick bush which would hide him and the umbrella, but through which he could point the umbrella, like a gun, at Pradeep.

Some time passed and then a few deer came down to drink at the waterhole and so did a few wild boar. Some monkeys, chattering madly, scampered down to the water, too, their furry heads turning to look in all directions. It was obvious that all the animals were rather nervous.

After another twenty minutes or so, they heard the peacocks' raucous cry for help, and shortly after that a few of them came down to the waterhole. The boys tensed in their positions.

Pradeep fired two shots in quick succession, killing two peacocks, left his gun on the ground near the bush where he had been hiding, and ran to the waterhole to pick up the birds.

'Hands up, or I'll shoot!' shouted Rohan in a stentorian voice. 'I have you covered.'

Startled, Pradeep looked up in fear towards the bushes where Rohan was. He did not recognize Rohan's voice. He saw what he thought was a gun pointing out of the bush at him, and promptly gave up all thought of trying to get to his own gun, which was lying four and a half metres away. In any event, it was unloaded since he had fired both cartridges at the birds. He raised his hands quickly in the air, assuming that he had been caught by one of the men belonging to the Conservation.

Just then, Nimal and Hunter rushed out of hiding.

Hunter, encouraged by Nimal, leapt on Pradeep, growling ferociously, and knocked him down. Nimal promptly pounced on him and Rohan ran out to join them. Together the boys and Hunter managed to hold Pradeep down, and Pradeep, who was shocked to see the boys, and not men as he had assumed, did not resist or shout out.

They trussed him up with Rohan's length of rope so that he could not move. Rohan picked up Pradeep's gun and, in front of Pradeep, loaded it with the cartridges he found in the man's pocket and put the extra cartridges into his own pockets. Pradeep tried to protest that it was dangerous, but a snarl from Hunter and a threatening look from Nimal who pretended he would set Hunter on him, made him stop in a hurry.

Both boys were used to handling guns for target practice, as they had been trained both in school, and by their fathers. So far they had never had to use a gun on the animals, but whenever they went into the CH section of the Conservation, where the more dangerous animals lived, they always took a gun, as well as a tranquillizer gun, with them. It was a necessary precaution if an animal became dangerous, and important for them to know how to scare it away and protect themselves. Their parents insisted that all four kids, in fact, should know how to handle a gun, including the tranquillizer guns used by the staff of the Conservation, since the children spent so much time in the jungle.

Rohan moved behind Pradeep so that the man could not see what he was doing, and set the safety trigger on the gun so that it could not go off by accident.

He winked at Nimal, who was glaring at Pradeep with deep loathing, and then joined him and Hunter. He pointed the gun at Pradeep.

'Be careful with that gun,' begged Pradeep anxiously. 'It could go off by accident and then someone'll get hurt.'

'Well, the only person who's likely to get hurt is you,' said Rohan callously.

'And, frankly speaking, we really don't care,' added Nimal angrily. 'How *dare* you come into our Conservation and kill the birds? You'll be going to jail for a long, long time.'

'How did you boys get free?' asked Pradeep, looking at Rohan. 'You were all tied up.'

'Never mind that,' said Rohan impatiently. 'We don't have time to waste answering your questions. But if you give us the information we want, and quickly, we'll do our best not to let the gun go off by mistake.' He waved it carelessly at Pradeep who cringed in fear and pleaded with him, again, to put it away.

'Oh, shut up, man,' growled Rohan. 'Just tell us what we want to know. Fast!'

'Well, if you think I'm going to give information to you kids, you'd better think again,' began Pradeep in a poor attempt at bravado.

Rohan interrupted him rudely. 'Look, man – I'm getting angrier – if possible – and if I lose my temper you'll be in major trouble. Nimal, could you get Hunter to give him a few bites? Perhaps that'll stop him from thinking we don't mean what we say.'

Nimal whispered something in Hunter's ear and Hunter, growling ferociously, grabbed hold of Pradeep's foot.

Pradeep cried out immediately. 'I give up, I give up. Call that dog off me. I'll tell you whatever you want to know.' He was totally cowed by now. What with the gun, these tough boys, and the fierce dog, he was in a really tight spot.

'Hunter, *release him!*' said Nimal, and Hunter immediately let go of Pradeep's foot but stayed close to the man, growling ominously.

'That's better,' said Rohan darkly. 'Now, where's the pickup spot?'

'It's near the small waterhole close to the main road, the one that's dried up,' said Pradeep hastily.

The main road leading to the Conservation ran parallel to the northern wall which fenced in the area. The waterhole he referred to was the only one so close to the road. It had a few large trees and a lot of thick bushes surrounding it, but there was no water in it any longer.

'And what was the plan?' asked Nimal. 'How were you going to be picked up?'

'The boss was going to pick us up by helicopter,' said Pradeep, who was now anxious to give these dangerous boys all the information they wanted, so that they would stop pointing the gun at him. 'He would hover above the spot, let down a rope for us to hang on to, and then lift us over the wall.'

There was an electric fence on top of the wall, which would prevent anyone from climbing over.

'Then what?' asked Rohan. 'How were you going to get away? Was he going to draw you up into the helicopter?'

'No, he would drop us into some thick bushes by the side of the road, and someone was going to pick us up in a car,' said Pradeep.

'Good. Now, how would you know it was *your* pickup car? That road is a fairly large highway, and even late at night there are quite a few cars using it,' said Nimal.

'And what time is the car expected?' continued Rohan.

'We'd know it was our car because it would stop near the pickup spot on the edge of the road,' said Pradeep to Nimal, 'and the driver would get out and pretend that he was checking something in the boot of his car. Chand and I would then quietly sneak into the back seat, and the driver would take off. And, there's no fixed time,' he continued, looking at

Rohan, 'because we don't know what could hold up traffic, so we just wait till the car arrives – any time after 12:30 a.m.'

'Isn't your boss scared that his helicopter will be seen by someone who would report it as unusual?' asked Nimal curiously.

'No, he wouldn't lift us over the wall until he had checked to see that no cars were in sight, and then it would take all of two minutes. He can see quite far from the helicopter and the road curves a lot. Now, please stop pointing that gun at me,' he begged. 'I've told you all I know.'

'One more thing,' said Nimal, 'how will your boss know that it's you and Chand at the waterhole and not some of the Conservation men who have spotted him?'

'Once we hear the helicopter overhead, we have to flash a torch three times rapidly, and the boss will know it's us,' said Pradeep.

'Okay,' said Rohan, 'I guess we'll leave it at that for now. The police can get all the details and information out of you about the rest of your network when you're taken to jail. Nimal, gag him so that he can't shout to Chand for help; he has a nice red scarf which should do the trick.'

'Sure thing,' said Nimal cheerfully, 'and with the greatest of pleasure. If you try and protest,' he continued pleasantly to Pradeep, 'I'm positive that Hunter will be only too willing to give you a few bites in a juicy spot.'

He set to work, and Pradeep was too scared to protest in any way.

In the meantime, Rohan beeped Anu on the walkie-talkie.

'Anu, come in. Over.'

'Rohan, thank goodness. What's happening? Over.'

'We got Pradeep. Over.'

'Great job, guys! Over,' said Anu excitedly.

'Where are the two of you? Over,' asked Rohan.

'We're just fifteen minutes from home – perfect timing. Over.'

'Good, here's the info,' said Rohan in low tones. He quickly gave Anu the location of the pickup point and also told her about the plans the crooks had made to get away.

'Anu, suggest to one of the adults that, perhaps, some of the police could hide near the pickup spot and catch Chand if he's not caught before he's lifted over the wall. Also they may be able to catch the driver of the pickup car, too – he's expected to be there after 12:30 midnight. Over.'

'Right,' said Anu eagerly, 'and if the police send a chopper or two, perhaps they'll also be able to capture the big boss in his chopper. Over.'

'Great idea,' said Rohan. 'Right. I think we're in good shape now. Let me know within the next five minutes if you have trouble finding any adults, because if we don't hear from you, we'll assume that things are okay at your end. In the meantime, Nimal, Hunter and I are going to look for Chand; we'll try and scare him into running to the pickup point early, so that he can't kill any more birds. Oh, also, we're leaving Pradeep here – he's tied securely and also gagged, so there's no need to leave Hunter here to guard him. Suggest that a couple of men come and fetch him – after all, we don't want any wild animals getting to him first, do we? Over.'

'Righto, chief,' said Anu with a chuckle. 'We'll call you and give you an update once we know whom we can reach. Good luck with Chand, but please take care. He's much tougher than Pradeep. Anything else? Over.'

'Just one more thing: if you take longer than ten minutes, try not to panic if you don't receive a response from me when you call. We may be near Chand by then, and unable to talk even in a whisper. If I can, I'll just beep you back in reply to say that we're all right, and we'll call you as soon as possible. Okay? That's it, then. Good luck to the two of you – you sure made excellent time. Hope the APs are home. Over and out.'

He grinned at Nimal, then turned to Pradeep and said, 'Well, you'll soon be out of your misery and in the comfortable confines of a jailhouse. So we'll say goodbye and leave you to meditate on your sins in peace.'

'That should give him lots of pleasure, but perhaps not enough time,' said Nimal with a laugh.

Pradeep could do nothing but glare at the two boys.

The boys placed the dead peacocks in the bag near Pradeep; then, picking up the umbrella and taking the gun they set off, with Hunter, for the second waterhole which Chand was going to cover, since they assumed he would have finished with the first one.

CHAPTER 18

Peter Takes Charge

Anu and Gina reached their home and found that none of the adults had returned yet. However, there was a message on the answering machine from their dad to say that their car had broken down and they would be in by around 11 p.m. It was now 10 o'clock. Mr. and Mrs. Collins were also with the Patels.

Anu promptly called her father on his mobile telephone.

'Dad, it's Anu! I know you're stuck, since we just got the message on the answering machine.' She briefly updated him on the situation.

'Anu,' said Mr. Patel quickly, 'Peter and Mike have both been in touch with me. Peter's at home and has been trying to contact you kids. He tried the cave, but found you were not there, so he went back home, hoping to hear from someone as to where you were. He knew you could not contact him if he was wandering around the Conservation since you don't have mobiles. You have all done a great job so far – congrats. But I think it would be a good idea to contact Peter and Mike now and ask them to take charge. Those crooks sound very dangerous.'

'Sure, Dad,' said Anu, 'will do right away. I'll call Peter and see what he wants us to do.'

'Good girl,' said Mr. Patel. 'Everyone sends love. Tell Peter to keep us informed. I will call him in about fifteen minutes and get details of where you will all be so that I can join you there, with the others. Bye for now.'

'Bye, Dad,' said Anu, 'and Gina says hello and bye, too. Give our love to everyone.' She hung up the phone and quickly dialled Peter's mobile telephone.

'Anu,' said a relieved Peter at the other end. 'Where are you folk? What's been happening?'

'Peter, we have so much to tell you,' said Anu excitedly. 'Where do you want us to meet? We're at home – just us two girls.'

'I'll be over in a jiffy,' said Peter, 'Are the boys okay?'

'Yeah, they were fine half an hour ago,' said Anu.

'Good,' said Peter, 'I have the Jeep. Stay where you are and, do you think you could find me something to eat? I've been too anxious to eat anything, but now I'm starving.'

Anu laughed. It was great that Peter was back and would take charge. It had been fun doing things all on their own, but she was nervous as the men had guns and appeared to be quite ruthless.

'We'll find something for you Pete,' she said. 'See you soon.'

The girls raided the well-stocked fridge, quickly put out some food, and by the time it was ready, they heard the crunch of wheels on the driveway, and ran out to welcome Peter.

He hugged them both, and they pulled him into the house. As they ate, they updated him on the events of that night, leaving out what happened earlier, because they wanted to help the boys as soon as possible.

'We'll tell you the whole story later,' said Anu, as Peter listened in astonishment to her tale of what the boys meant to do, where the pickup point was, and the scheme of how the crooks were aiming to escape.

'I'm amazed at the way all of you have handled everything so far,' said Peter. 'Okay, I'll wait to hear the whole story once we've dealt with the crooks. Now, let me think for a few minutes and make a couple of calls to the Mallicks and DeSouzas, so that I can get a few of the others to assist. Then, we'll all set out for the pickup spot. I've already contacted Mike and he'll call back in fifteen minutes. He's been searching for you frantically in the vicinity of your cave, and was relieved to hear you were all right.'

Peter made his calls and some rapid arrangements. Monica Mallick would call the police and arrange matters with them. Anil and Ben were already on their way to join Peter and the girls at the house. Along the way, Ben would alert some of the other Conservation staff, a couple of whom would try to get to the waterholes where Chand was supposed to go, in case the boys needed help. Others would join them at the pickup point as soon as they could. Mike called in, was updated, and planned to meet them at the pickup spot, too.

Someone would meet the police at the gate to the Conservation and take some of them to the pickup point outside the Centre; more policemen would go, with another staff person, to the waterhole where the boys had left Pradeep, and collect him.

'The arrangements sound fantastic,' said Anu and Gina, who were listening open-mouthed to Peter's rapid instructions.

Just then Mr. Patel called Peter, who updated him briefly.

'You're so thorough, Peter,' said Anu in admiration. 'I'm *so* glad you're with us now.'

Just then they heard the screeching of tires as Anil's Jeep whipped into the driveway and came to a halt outside the house. They all ran out.

Anil and Ben took out their guns and rope from the back of the Jeep. Peter collected his gun from his Jeep, and then looked at the girls a little anxiously, but with a twinkle in his eyes.

'I guess the two of you want to come along,' he said. 'You're not too sleepy or scared, are you?'

'Of course we're coming,' chorused the girls indignantly.

'And I'm wide awake,' added Gina, opening her eyes wide and glaring at Peter.

'I figured,' he said with a laugh, 'that we couldn't possibly leave you behind, and,' he continued, turning to the two men, 'they'd be safer with us any way. Okay, let's go.' They set off. 'Anu, could you try and reach Rohan on the walkie-talkie, please, and see if we can get an update of where they are?'

'Right,' said Anu.

She took the walkie-talkie out of her knapsack. 'Rohan, Rohan, come in, please. Over.' There was no reply. She tried a few more times, but did not get even a beep in response.

'I'm sure they're right in the middle of something,' said Anu at last, when she had tried about six or seven times, unsuccessfully. 'Do you think we should go to the waterhole where Chand was supposed to be, Peter?' she asked anxiously.

Peter and the two men discussed the situation quickly, and then agreed that they would still go straight to the pickup spot.

'From the way you described Chand, Anu,' said Peter, 'I doubt he'll be caught that easily and will probably try to get away to the pickup point and hide there. Also, don't forget some of our folks are already on their way to the waterholes where Chand and the boys may be, and can help there if necessary.'

'If I know those two boys,' said Anil, 'they won't take foolish chances – as long as Rohan keeps his temper. Perhaps they'll just try and frighten the man to make a run for it. After all, they know he's a tough character.'

'You're probably right, Anil. Now, we'd better go softly,' said Peter, 'just in case we bump into Chand.'

They stopped talking, and wound their way along the trail, making straight for the waterhole near the wall. Once Peter's mobile telephone beeped softly, and they stopped so that he could answer it. It was Monica – she informed them that the police were on their way and would be in place by 11:30 p.m. She also said that all the other staff had called her, too, so that there were not too many calls beeping on Peter's telephone, and they were either in place to meet the police or on their way to their various assignments, as agreed.

'Also, watch out for a possible helicopter chase,' she added, with a small laugh. 'The police are landing two of their helicopters near the gates and will wait till the men have been lifted over the wall. Then they'll give chase and try to capture the crooks' helicopter. I'm sure the kids will enjoy that part of it – just like a Bond movie. Are the girls okay?'

'Thanks, Monica,' said Peter. 'Sounds like you've covered everything from that end. If any of the men call you, just give them an update, please. Yeah, the girls are fine. Anything else?'

'Yes, tell everyone to come back to the Patels' house. I just called the DeSouzas, and we agreed that everyone will be dying to hear details of the capture and will want to celebrate – no matter how late the hour. We'll start preparations for a feast. Many of the folk from the CH are also coming over to help, and, of course, listen to the tale.'

Peter laughed, 'Superfab, Monica. You can bet we'll all be celebrating. Tell the others when they call in. Thanks. See you later.'

He rang off and told everyone the latest news.

'Your wives are preparing a feast for us when we return,' he said to the two men. 'Let's hope things go smoothly and we catch those crooks fast.'

They made their way to the waterhole without meeting anyone. When they got there, Peter made the girls stand quietly in a safe spot, while he, Ben and Anil scouted the area. They did not discover anyone else there yet.

Peter suggested that the girls climb a tall tamarind tree with thick, bushy branches that would hide them totally from sight. It was right next to the wall and they would be able to see all the action taking place around the waterhole, in the air and also on the other side of the wall. On the other hand, they would be quite safe from gunshots and any rough-housing that might occur. Everyone was tense with excitement.

'Also, Anu,' said Peter, 'you'd better give the walkie-talkie to Ben, so that if Rohan does call, Ben can talk to him and then alert us on the mobile.'

Anu handed it over and the girls climbed up the tree.

'I'll just call Mike and Gune who are to meet us here,' said Peter to the two men, 'and then we'll go into hiding.'

'Mike,' said Peter, a few seconds later, 'we're in place. The girls are safe in the tamarind tree next to the wall, with Ben below to protect them if necessary. There's no one else here at present. I'll be in the thick bush nearest their tree. When you get here, first beep me on my mobile and when I beep back, come and join me and I'll give you further instructions. You and Gune are so quiet in the jungle that I may take you for the enemy if you creep up without warning me first. I'll have my earpiece on so the beeper doesn't go off loudly and you'd better do the same. Oh, and by the way, Anil will be right opposite me, just in case you think *he's* the crook. I know you two guys have eyes like hawks.'

'Right, Pete – I'll update Gune,' said Mike. 'We're about ten minutes away. See you soon.'

Peter turned to Anil and Ben. 'They'll be here around 11:15. I wonder when things will actually start happening, and I wish I knew what the boys were doing, and if they've met up with Mano and Sanjay yet. Those two should be quite close to the third waterhole by now, but I don't want to take the risk of calling them on the mobile in case Chand is around and hears it.'

The men moved to their appointed places, guns handy and ready for action at any moment. They were all anxious to capture the crooks who had been the cause of so much grief to their beloved Conservation.

CHAPTER 19

Things Get Hotter

The boys and Hunter were trailing Chand. They had gone to the second waterhole which Chand was supposed to cover, but found no one there.

'I guess he's moved on to the third waterhole,' said Nimal. 'I don't see any signs of a bird being shot here, and we didn't hear the gun, so that's some consolation at least.'

'Yes, and we'd better be really cautious as we go towards the waterhole,' said Rohan. 'What do you think we should do when we get there?'

'Well, Chand is unlikely to be frightened as easily as Pradeep,' said Nimal thoughtfully, 'and I doubt he'll hesitate to fire his gun at us – especially if he thinks we're Conservation men. He had no hesitation in shooting Haren. So I think we should be the ones to shoot first or at least pretend to.'

'Hmmm, that's true,' said Rohan, 'but I don't like the idea of actually shooting someone.' He pondered the situation for a moment and then continued, 'Perhaps, as you suggested, we can pretend to shoot at him, but shoot up into the air or deliberately away from him if we know where he is.'

'Yeah, and then if we can make him believe that there are more than the two of us he may panic and try to run away to the pickup spot,' said Nimal excitedly.

'Okay,' said Rohan, 'I think I'll put the walkie-talkie away now as it's unlikely that I'll get a chance to answer it once we get to that waterhole. The girls will know we're in the thick of something if we don't answer.'

'Yeah,' said Nimal, 'we can call them once we have chased Chand away from this waterhole.'

'Also, let's make sure that neither of us, nor Hunter, ever put ourselves in the way of Chand's gun,' said Rohan. 'We won't be helping anyone if we get ourselves shot and, in fact, we may jeopardize the others if we're caught or hurt, and someone has to rescue us.'

After a few minutes of brainstorming, they came up with a good scheme as to how they could confuse Chand. Taking shortcuts known only to those who lived on the Conservation, they moved swiftly but quietly, and reached the waterhole in record time. They met no one on the way.

There were a number of animals at the waterhole, making quite a bit of noise. Hunter growled softly and was immediately shushed by Nimal, while both boys quickly hid in a thick bush, taking Hunter with them. They pulled out their binoculars and searched carefully for any signs of Chand or his yellow shirt. It was quite dark though, and a cloud was covering the moon – they could not see a thing. They were just about to move out of their place and go to another spot, when they suddenly heard a soft cough to their right. Hunter growled again and the boys knew at once that it had to be Chand. Nimal bent down and whispered to Hunter to be quiet and the dog obeyed immediately.

The boys then focused their binoculars on the bushes from where they had heard the noise. Was it Chand or was it one of the men from the Conservation?

The moon came out from behind a cloud. 'I see something yellowish,' mouthed Nimal in Rohan's ear, a few minutes later. 'I'm sure it's Chand.' Rohan spotted the man, too, and nodded his head in agreement.

As planned, the boys parted. Nimal, carrying the umbrella, slipped away with Hunter to the left, heading for some thick bushes opposite

Chand's hiding place, and untied one of the lengths of rope he had wrapped around his waist. He planned to fasten it to some bushes a couple of metres away from the one he would hide in and would, on cue, pull the rope vigorously and shake the bushes so that Chand thought there was someone hiding there. Then he would move to another spot a bit further on and do the same thing. He would set up both ropes before he signalled Rohan that he was ready for action.

Rohan, with the gun and two extra cartridges easily accessible, stayed where he was. He would wait for Nimal to shake the first set of bushes gently, and then their plan would take off. Chand coughed again. It was evident that he had no fear of being caught.

A few minutes later Nimal was hiding in the first spot, all set to go. Instructing Hunter to stay quiet for now, he shook the other bushes gently as though in a breeze and Rohan saw it at once.

'Come out of there or I'll shoot,' yelled Rohan in a bass tone. 'I can see you – you in the yellow shirt.' As he said this, he quickly moved away from his spot, and further away from Chand.

Nimal called out next, in as deep a voice as he could manage, 'I have my gun trained on you, so don't do anything stupid.' He pulled on the rope as he spoke and the bushes rustled rapidly.

Chand, who had frozen for a second when Rohan called out, recovered rapidly and picking up his gun as he stepped away from his bush, he fired straight at the bushes being shaken by Nimal.

Rohan called out again from his new spot behind a large tree. He stepped out from behind it and fired a shot into the tree next to Chand, taking immediate cover behind his tree again. Chand's reaction with his gun was faster this time, but as he had been concentrating on the bushes Nimal was shaking, his second bullet was aimed at least a metre or more to Rohan's left. He, too, moved away from his bush since he did not want to be a sitting target for anyone.

Then Nimal yelled again, this time pulling on the second rope he had tied to the other bushes. Rohan fired his second shot, this time two metres over Chand's head, and quickly reloaded his gun as he moved behind another large tree.

Chand panicked. He could not tell how many people were around the waterhole, and he knew that he would be caught unless he acted fast. He tried to reload his gun, looking in his pockets for cartridges, but found none. Whirling around, he looked for his bags which held the cartridges. Unfortunately, in his dismay at the unexpected situation, he had moved about six and a half metres away from his bags. He turned and ran towards them, but when he was three metres away, Rohan shot a cartridge right next to the bags, and Chand, in a frenzy of fear, left his bags and disappeared into the jungle. The boys could hear him running away rapidly.

Nimal and Rohan, encouraged by this flight, followed up with a few yells, and then Nimal got Hunter to bark loudly, and they made a great deal of noise so that Chand would think he was being chased by a number of men. Soon, they heard nothing at all, and Hunter stopped barking.

As the boys and Hunter met near the edge of the waterhole, they heard rapid footsteps coming towards them, and promptly hid in the bushes. However, as they peered out cautiously, they saw that it was only Mano and Sanjay. The boys came out of hiding and greeted them joyfully. The men were relieved to see them safe – they had been worried when they heard the gunshots and shouting. They listened eagerly to what had occurred.

Then Sanjay updated the boys on what had been happening since they last talked to the girls. The boys were glad to hear that Peter and Mike were now right in the thick of things, and that the girls were safe.

After a brief discussion, the four of them agreed to set Hunter on the trail and see if they could find out where Chand was headed.

'I've a feeling he may go straight to the pickup point,' said Rohan. 'He left his things in the bush since he couldn't collect them, and I doubt he'll bother to come back for them. He thinks this place is surrounded.'

'Yeah,' said Nimal, 'he'll try and hide around there so that he's safe. But I think someone should go to the cave in case he goes back to pick up the transmitter and warn the boss to be extra careful.'

'Well, why don't Sanjay and I go to the cave?' suggested Mano. 'I think there are enough staff at the pickup spot to deal with Chand if he goes there, and we'll take his gear with us.' He collected Chand's bags from the bush.

'Good idea,' said Sanjay. 'We just got a call from Mike to say that he and Gune had reached the pickup point, too. So now there are five of them to deal with Chand if necessary. Also,' he continued with a grin, 'I've a feeling you two boys would rather be in on the action at the pickup point, and after all the detective work you kids have done, you certainly deserve it.'

'Thanks, yaar,' said Rohan gratefully. 'We'd really like to be there.'

'I'll call Pete on his mobile and tell him that he may have some action at that end fairly soon and also that you two boys are on your way to join him. Also, don't worry about trying to contact the girls on the walkie-talkie, they're safe,' said Mano.

'Actually, it may be a good idea for you boys to take my mobile,' said Sanjay, handing it over to Rohan. 'Since Mano and I are going on the same trail, we don't need two units. Once you figure out which direction Chand is headed in, call Pete and tell him where the two of you are. Then get further instructions from him as to what he wants you to do so that no one runs into any danger.'

'Great idea,' said Rohan. 'We'll make sure we contact him before Chand gets too close to the waterhole, so that we don't jeopardize any of his plans.'

'We'll call Pete right away,' said Mano, 'and warn him to keep the line clear for you two. It'll take anyone at least 25 minutes to get to the waterhole from here, even if they're in a hurry. But don't delay too long before you call him. We'll see you guys later.'

The boys gave them directions to the cave and how to get in, then waving goodbye, they set Hunter the task of tracking Chand.

Hunter soon picked up the trail, and the boys followed him as he sniffed his way along. They knew Chand was not too close or else Hunter would have been growling.

'Chand seems to have been following the trail pretty closely, yaar,' muttered Nimal, after a few minutes, 'and I think he's definitely on the way to the pickup spot. What do you think?'

'Yeah, I believe you're right,' said Rohan, 'but the next fork will tell us for sure.'

The trail was easy enough to follow because Chand had left footprints in many places where the ground was still rather damp.

'He doesn't know this jungle very well,' said Rohan, 'not the way all of us at the Conservation do – and thank goodness for that.'

'Ah, here we are at the fork,' said Nimal as the trail branched left and right.

However, the ground was hard and dry at that spot, and Hunter sniffed around for a moment, before he picked up the scent again, and turned right. A few moments later, the boys saw more footprints.

'He's definitely on his way to the waterhole,' said Rohan excitedly. 'I think we'd better call Peter now, because Chand will get there in about fifteen minutes, and we're probably ten minutes behind him.'

'Sounds good,' said Nimal, stopping Hunter. 'It's better for us to know what he wants us to do before Chand reaches the waterhole and Pete can't talk to us.'

The boys called Peter. Both of them put their ears close to the earpiece of the telephone so that they would not miss a word. Peter was very relieved to hear from them and they quickly updated him on the situation.

'Right, boys,' he said, softly, 'you've done a great job. Do you know if Chand has a loaded gun?'

'He doesn't,' said Rohan. 'He didn't have time to reload it – and unless he finds more cartridges in his pockets, he's out of luck.'

'Great,' said Peter. 'I have an idea which I hope will work. Do you think one of you could trail the man to his exact location, and then come and tell me – perhaps you, Rohan – while Nimal controls Hunter and keeps him absolutely quiet?'

'Sure,' said Rohan excitedly. 'Will do.'

'And, Nimal,' continued Peter, 'I'd like you and Hunter to join Mike in his hideout, as he's the most silent tracker in our team, and await my signal. I'll tip him off that you'll be joining him. He already has my instructions.'

'Okey-dokey, chief,' said Nimal gleefully.

Peter told the boys exactly where he, Mike and the others were hiding and then rang off. Things were heating up!

When they were five minutes away from the waterhole, the boys stopped. Hunter looked up at them inquiringly. He could smell that nasty man quite strongly now.

Giving each other the thumbs up signal, the boys parted, each setting off to follow their instructions.

Nimal and Hunter soon joined Mike, who was in a dense bush from where he could watch the waterhole, but a little distance away from it. This would enable the staff to move around the waterhole easily without being seen by someone hidden in the undergrowth right at the edge of the waterhole. Nimal and Mike greeted each other with a handshake, and Hunter was told to keep very quiet. In low tones, Mike instructed Nimal on what they had to do once they received Peter's signal.

In the meantime, Rohan trailed Chand. There were no footprints to be seen, but Rohan was an excellent tracker and was able to find other signs that told him someone had blundered their way through the jungle. He kept a sharp lookout, and when he was about ten to twelve metres away from the waterhole, he stopped. Taking out his binoculars, he scanned the area, looking for a yellow shirt, some movement or sound which would tell him where the crook was hiding.

Suddenly he heard a small sound to his right, a few metres ahead of him. It was someone clearing his throat quietly. Focusing his binoculars on the bushes in that area, Rohan spotted a yellow shirt in the thick forsythia bush. He grinned to himself and thought, 'It's a good hiding spot for you man, since the bush is also yellow, but your throat gave you away.'

Once Rohan knew Chand was there, it was easy to follow his movements. Chand was ensconced in the bush with his gun on the ground beside him. He was fishing in his pockets and pulled out a torch, which he laid down. He looked over his shoulder occasionally, but Rohan was well hidden and his clothing blended into the jungle so perfectly, that Chand could not see him at all.

After a couple of minutes, obviously hearing no signs of a chase, and with nothing else to disturb him, Chand appeared to relax a bit. He set about checking all the other pockets in his jeans. He found a packet of sandwiches, which he placed beside him, but did not seem to find anything else of interest.

'I guess he's looking for cartridges,' thought Rohan to himself, 'and lucky for us he hasn't found any. Well, it's 11:30 now, and I'd better go and report to Pete.'

He moved away from his hiding place, and made his way silently to where Peter was hidden.

'Good to see you, Rohan,' said Peter, greeting him with a whisper, as Rohan came up. 'Any luck?'

'Yeah – good news,' said Rohan softly.

He quickly told Peter where Chand was. Peter was delighted to hear that Chand had no ammunition in his gun. He immediately got on the telephone to Mike and informed him of this, and instructed him and Nimal to carry out the next stage of the plan.

Mike, Nimal and Hunter set out from their spot and were soon a few metres away from the bush where Chand was hiding. They were all so silent that Chand had no clue they were just behind him.

At Mike's signal, Nimal whispered to Hunter, who could smell the enemy again.

Barking loudly, Hunter charged the bush with Mike and Nimal right behind him. Chand, who got a severe shock, immediately picked up his gun to hit out with it. However, Mike, with a swift karate kick, knocked the gun out of his hands. Nimal jumped on Chand's back and was thrown off, but rose instantly and ran to help Mike. Hunter joined in the fray with great enthusiasm, taking his chance to give Chand a few nips, and the man cried out in anger and pain. He put up a good fight, but was no match for Mike, who caught his arm and threw him over his hip to land on the ground with a hard thump. Chand lay gasping for breath, and before he could recover, Mike and Nimal had pounced on him. Then, as more staff converged on him from various points, Chand gave up. He knew it was over and that he had lost.

'Boy! Mike,' said Rohan as everyone paused to draw breath, 'I sure wish I was as good as you at Karate. That was a superb throw.'

'Just fantabulous,' agreed Nimal admiringly, 'the way you threw him over your hip – awesome! I can't wait to get my green belt next.'

Mike grinned at the boys, shrugging off their praise and looking rather embarrassed.

Chand, seeing both Rohan and Nimal, glared at them and spat out, 'How did you get free? And get that horrible dog away from me,' he continued, kicking out at Hunter who was trying to get in another good nip.

Nimal called Hunter off and said, 'Another one bites the dust! Like we're going to tell you how we got free,' he added scathingly.

'Bind him fast and gag him,' said Peter to a couple of the men, 'and let's get ready for the next bit of action.'

Chand swore profoundly, but was soon silenced by the gag. The men were none too gentle with him either, and he was bound and placed at the bottom of the tree where the girls and Ben were, with Hunter standing over him.

The guards at the gate were quickly updated via mobile telephone, and they, in turn, would alert the police helicopters to be ready for take-off as soon as they received a signal from Mike, who would be co-ordinating the next stage of things.

CHAPTER 20

Hurrah for the JEACs!

Peter picked up the torch and remained near the edge of the waterhole, Rohan beside him. All the others – except for Anil who stayed on the ground in case something went wrong, and Peter and Rohan needed assistance – climbed up the tree so that they, too, could watch what happened on the other side of the wall. The girls were delighted to see Nimal again, and soon everyone was comfortably seated on the wide branches of the tree. There was more than enough room for the crowd.

'Now, quiet everyone,' whispered Mike who was also in the tree. 'The chopper may arrive any moment, and you know how voices can carry in the jungle.'

They had heard helicopters a while before, but knew that they belonged to the police, since the guard had called Peter on his mobile telephone as soon as the police landed near the gates.

Everything was in place for the big capture. There was no noise for a little while, and only the drone of an occasional car on the road could be heard. They heard the trumpeting of elephants in the distance.

Then, after about ten minutes, the sound of a helicopter was heard. The children scanned the skies with their binoculars and saw a helicopter approaching from the north. It had no lights on, was moving quite slowly and, a short time later, it was hovering over the waterhole.

Nobody made a sound. Peter flashed the torch, on and off, at the helicopter. Once, twice, thrice! Immediately a rope was thrown down from the helicopter, right in the middle of the dry waterhole.

Rohan ran out from the bushes and, as the others watched eagerly, he caught hold of the rope and was lifted up by the helicopter.

Over the wall and way over the electric fence went Rohan, clinging on to the rope. Peter and Anil joined the others in the tree, and as everybody watched with bated breath, Rohan was lowered to the ground on the other side of the wall, right into some dense bushes. They could not see him at all – just the helicopter and the rope.

As Rohan touched the ground, he quickly wrapped the end of the rope around the trunk of a stout bush and tied it, hoping the bush would be strong enough to resist the pull of the helicopter.

The helicopter jerked up and down above the bushes, but could not dislodge the rope.

As the group in the tree watched in amazement, they heard the sound of two helicopters moving fast.

'Those should be the police choppers arriving now,' said Peter. 'Looks like the crooks are stuck.'

Sure enough, the two police helicopters came into sight seconds later, and using megaphones, ordered the crook's helicopter to land on the highway, saying that they had guns trained on it and would shoot if necessary.

The boss had no choice but to land as commanded since the helicopter was secured firmly, and he could not free himself. One of the police helicopters landed, too, and three officers ran towards the crook's machine. The boss had no gun with him and he raised his hands angrily.

'Well, well, well – it's Raaju the great. Himself, and not a picture!' said the police officer-in-charge. 'Why didn't we guess that you might be involved in this racket?'

He signalled to the other policemen to tie the man up. Raaju was then placed in the police helicopter, which took off to return to the gates of the Conservation.

Another policeman, obviously a pilot, climbed into the abandoned helicopter and flew it off to the police headquarters.

The other policemen came out of their various hiding places at that point and Rohan waved to everyone up in the tree. They were all cheering madly.

'Quick thinking, Rohan,' praised Peter. 'Stay there until the police have bagged the whole gang. Once they're caught, we'll meet you at the gates. There'll be enough vehicles to get us back to your place.'

Rohan and the policemen went back into hiding.

'But what about the other cars on the road? I haven't seen any at all for a while,' asked Anu suddenly.

'Don't worry, Anu,' said Mike, 'I'm sure the police have already set up a roadblock on either side of this stretch of road and that's why we haven't seen any cars so far. When they clear the roadblock they'll tell the folk some story or the other so that the driver of the pickup car for the crooks won't be scared away. Also, the curve in the road would have prevented any oncoming traffic from seeing what actually happened on the road unless they were very close by.'

Everyone fell silent again. No cars came by for a while. Then, about ten minutes later, two police cars passed each other, going in opposite directions. Behind these were several other cars.

'I guess your assumption was correct, Mike,' said Ben. 'We should have some more fun in a short while.'

Everyone watched eagerly as the number of cars on the road lessened, and soon there was only the occasional car passing by once more. Then a large, black Mercedes Benz came by, driving relatively slowly given the fact that it was on a highway.

It stopped right opposite them, just off the highway, in front of the bushes where the policemen were hidden. The driver got out and went to the boot of his car and opened it, pretending to look for something, and the policemen charged out of the bushes, guns at the ready and arrested him. The man did not have a chance to resist or get away.

He was also tied and placed in the back seat. A policeman drove the car and Rohan sat beside him. Then, followed by loud cheering from the tree, and barking from Hunter at the foot of the tree, the car drove to the gates of the Conservation.

Everyone descended from the tree hurriedly and, freeing Chand's feet so that he could walk, they quickly made their way to the gates.

What excitement there was! Sanjay and Mano were there, and Pradeep had been brought over, too. Mr. Patel and Mr. Collins were also at the gates, waiting to greet the children and the others. Peter spoke to the police officer-in-charge.

'We'll try and organize a court case in the next couple of days,' he said. 'We'll appoint a lawyer for the crooks if they wish for one. Of course if they choose to plead guilty and represent themselves, then it'll be a cut and dried case.'

'I have my doubts as to their pleading guilty, sir,' said the officer. 'As you know, their boss Raaju is that notorious gang leader we've come across before – he's extremely wily and very rich. He'll probably try to cook up a good story, and unless we have sound proof and one of his own men is willing to turn traitor to him and become a witness for us, he could get away.'

'Then, we should make sure that we persuade one of his men to witness on our behalf,' said Peter grimly, 'and I think the best one would be Pradeep, who seems to be a real wimp from what I've heard. Keep him apart from the others, and I'll come in and have a chat with him tomorrow morning. I have good, persuasive communication skills when it comes to crooks.'

'Right, sir,' said the officer with a grin. 'We'll make sure they're in separate jailhouses so that there's absolutely no chance of them talking to each other, and they'll also be heavily guarded.'

Peter nodded. He agreed to write up the case and bring the children, and anyone else directly involved, to the police station the next day so that they could discuss how best to ensure that the crooks were dealt with severely.

Congratulations flowed all around. Everyone wanted to hear the story, including the chowkidars at the gate. So the police officer-in-charge very kindly left two of his men to guard the gates and all the Conservation folk piled into vehicles and went back to the Patels' home.

The crooks were loaded into police vans. Pradeep was driven off in a separate car and he looked scared to death. They would be taken to the police station for questioning and to make their statements. Then they would be held in jail till the time of the court case.

It was well past 1 a.m. by then, but no one – not even little Gina – was the least bit sleepy.

'I guess it's all the excitement,' said Gina, hanging on to her father's arm as they got out of the car at home, 'and I'm starving!'

Everyone laughed, but had to admit that they were all very hungry, too. None of them had really had much dinner that night.

Mrs. Patel and the others greeted the group as they got out of the vehicles and swarmed into the house, laughing and chatting. The place was crowded with staff from the CH, too.

'Guess who's here, kids?' said Mrs. Patel nodding towards the living room.

The children rushed over.

'Bill,' yelled Nimal, charging across the room to shake the man's hand vigorously, 'it's simply great to see you. How's your leg?'

The others crowded around Bill, too, shaking his hand and welcoming him back.

'Much better, thanks. Your parents picked me up on the way back from their fundraiser,' said Bill with a laugh. 'They knew I was pining to be back here. But little did I know what sort of excitement was going on at this end.' He was beaming with delight.

'What about your leg?' said Anu. 'Are you sure you'll be able to manage here?'

'Of course,' said Bill, 'but who's this?' he continued as he saw Hunter. 'A newcomer to the family?'

Hunter was introduced and then Mrs. Patel called out.

'Food in the large dining room,' she said, 'so that we're all together.'

The table was loaded with delicious food and a large bowl, filled to capacity, was waiting for Hunter beside it. Hunter immediately started eating – he was as hungry as could be.

'Hope you don't mind us starting, too,' said Nimal hungrily eyeing the food. 'We haven't eaten in months!'

'Go ahead, son,' laughed his uncle. 'We'd hate you to drop down in a faint due to sheer hunger. Think of the crack it would make in the floor.'

'Also,' continued Peter, 'if you folk finish first, you can begin telling us your side of the story. A number of us have only heard bits and pieces, and some of us don't know it at all, except for what occurred in the last couple of hours. It would be great if we could hear the whole thing in order of occurrence, with everyone joining in at the appropriate places. That'll give me a clear picture of exactly what happened, and will also help me when I have to put a case together against those crooks tomorrow.'

'Also,' said Bill, 'I'm totally in the dark about everything that's happened since you kids came back, so I need every teeny, weeny detail, please.' He was thrilled to be back in his 'family' as he thought of the folk at the Conservation, and absolutely delighted that the crooks had been caught.

'Okay, JEACs,' said Rohan, as he and the others tucked into the delicious meal, 'eat up fast!'

'Why don't the rest of us also serve ourselves and get seated,' suggested Mrs. Collins, 'and then we will be ready to hear the children's story.'

The adults all moved into the dining room, and served themselves, too. Once everyone was served and seated, Rohan, who had nearly finished his meal, looked at Anu and said, 'Well, what about it, sis? You're the best storyteller, so why don't you start us off, and we'll each join in to tell our share of the story where required. However, we do need a narrator, and you're it.'

The whole room cheered; they were in high spirits and ready to cheer at the smallest thing.

'Go on, Anu,' encouraged her mother, 'you really do a good job.'

Blushing slightly, Anu consented to be the narrator. She finished her meal and took a couple of deep breaths.

'Once upon a time,' said Anu with a grin – and she began the tale.

She had a good, clear mind, and a storyteller's gift of narrative. Everyone listened, entranced.

The story unfolded gradually, the others joining in and linking up the entire tale.

'And so,' Anu concluded, 'our Conservation is now free of the anxiety caused by those horrible men, and our beloved peacocks are safe. I think we should give ourselves a rousing cheer. Here's to CONSERVATION!'

Led by Anu, the whole room cheered lustily till the roof rang, and Hunter joined in, barking madly.

'And here come Sunder and Sunderi to say, "Thank you, JEACs",' said Mike with a grin, as the two peacocks wandered into the room and, naturally, went up to Nimal and Hunter and settled down next to the dog.

'We leave you kids alone for a short time,' said Mr. Patel with a smile, 'and you get yourselves, and us, into all kinds of melodramatic situations. But,' he continued, looking at the children with love and pride glowing in his face, 'you've helped us solve a nasty case, and we are extremely proud of you. Thank you!'

Everyone gave the children a special cheer, and the JEACs felt satisfied that they had helped their beloved Conservation, and that the beautiful peacocks were safe from poachers.

'What's going to happen next?' asked Rohan, as Peter, Mike and Mr. Patel came over to talk to them.

'Well,' said Peter, 'we're going to need all the proof you folk have – the photographs, the drawing of the footprints and the various other clues you picked up, including the transmitter which we collected. No doubt we caught the crooks red-handed, but every little bit helps so that we have an open and shut case, and can put them away for a long, long time.'

'Do we have to go to court, as well, to ... to ... *tetsify*? That would be kind of neat,' asked Gina sleepily.

'It's *testify*, love,' said Mike gently, picking up the little girl who was yawning now and giving her a hug.

'Yes, of course you must be present,' said Peter. 'We can't possibly win the case without our star witnesses.'

The others grinned in satisfaction. Testify at a court case against the crooks was just what they would like. It would be a new experience.

'And don't forget to bring along your umbrella,' added Peter, who had been quite intrigued by it.

Of course everyone else wanted to see the umbrella, too, and it was brought out and examined by the others. Rohan gave a demonstration of how it worked, and the group was most impressed.

'It's ingenious!' said Peter. 'Do you think your friend's father would make some for my department? When some of us have to go about in disguise on some of our cases, it's easier to take a weapon that looks innocent compared to carting a gun around in a holster.'

'I could ask him,' said Rohan.

'Special treat for the children,' cried Vida and Yvette, as they came out of the kitchen, carrying something on a large tray between them.

'Oooh! It's an enormous, simply superfantabulous CHOCOLATE CAKE!' yelled Gina and Nimal together. Everyone roared with laughter, especially as Hunter also licked his lips and barked loudly when he got a whiff of the cake.

'It says "Congrats on a superb job, JEACs",' read Rohan, as Vida placed the cake on the table.

Once more the room erupted in cheers.

And as they enjoyed their cake – yes, Hunter, too – the JEACs felt proud to have been instrumental in saving the peacocks. It had been a grand adventure and – who knew – perhaps they would have more.

After all, as everyone knows – adventures come to the adventurous!

*   *   *

GLOSSARY

Word	Meaning
Acronym	A word formed from the initial letters of other words
Antiji	Aunt – 'ji' is added as a form of respect
APs	Aged Parents – acronym
Binocs	Binoculars – short form
Biscuits	Cookies
Boot of his car	The trunk of his car
Brekker	Breakfast – short form
CH	Conservationists' Heaven
Chevda	East Indian mixture of various grains and nuts
Chopper	Helicopter – short form, casual
Chowkidar	A watchman
Delish	Delicious – short form
Dhal	Lentils – a grain food
Dhoti/dhotis	A long piece of cloth worn by men, wrapped around their waist and between their legs
Egg bhujia	Scrambled eggs with onion, tomato and green chillies
English Lit	English Literature – short form
Exactimo	Exactly – fun usage
Germ/germs	Gentlemen – fun usage when saying 'ladies and germs'
Hindi	One of the languages of India
Hols	Holidays – short form (vacation)
Hon	Honey – short form
HP	Harmonious Paradise
Khana	Food – Hindi
Mater	Mother – Latin origin
Mes amis	My friends – French
Mince curry	Ground beef curry
Mobile phone	Cell phone
Moi	Me – French
Mon enfant	My child – French
Mummyji	Mother – 'ji' is added as a form of respect
Nawab	An important minister in the government of some East Indian states
Nineteen to the dozen	Talks a lot – idiom
No problemo	No problem – fun usage of word 'problem'

Word	Meaning
Parathas	A flat East Indian bread that you cook in a pan
Pater	Father – Latin origin
Rem acu tetigisti	You have touched the matter with a needle – Latin expression
Rotis	A type of flat round bread
Rupees	The unit of money used in India, Sri Lanka, and some other countries
Sahib	Used in India as a title of respect for a man
Situ	Situation – short form
Titbit	A small piece of tasty food (or information) – 'tidbit' in US English
Turban	A long piece of cloth wrapped around the head
Voilà	Expression used to call attention; to express satisfaction or approval – French
Yaar	Mate/Buddy – most often used in India by males

ABOUT THE AUTHOR

Amelia Lionheart has been writing for many years and is the published author of four books for children. She has a diploma in writing from the Institute of Children's Literature, Connecticut, USA.

Amelia, who has lived and worked in several countries, believes very strongly in the conservation of wildlife and, in particular, the protection of endangered species. She is convinced that awareness of this issue, when imbued in children at an early age, is a vital step towards saving our planet.

As a member of several nature/wildlife preservation organizations, including the Durrell Wildlife Conservation Trust, she invites children and their families to become involved with local zoos and conservation centres and to support their important work, both by creating awareness and fundraising. To encourage this, she created a group called the 'Junior Environmentalists and Conservationists' (the JEACs) in the first book of her JEACs' series, *Peacock Feathers*. In the other books, the JEACs travel to various countries, having adventures while enlarging their group and encouraging local children to start groups of JEACs in their own countries. As of November 2013, Amelia has four *real* groups of JEACs in Canada. The JEACs continue to evolve.

Amelia's other interests include environmental issues, volunteer work and fundraising. She believes that if people from different countries explore the diversity of cultures and learn from one another, they will discover that they have more similarities than dissimilarities. Many of these ideas are included in her books.

Please check out http://www.jeacs.com,
Amelia's website for children.